"I think he'll keep killing until he can get what he really wants—you."

"I know you probably think I should leave," she said, looking out the window, "but I refuse to allow the Composer to drive me from my home."

She hadn't heard him walk up behind her, but she felt his heat at her back. "As long as the Composer is out there, you're not safe. Which is why I'm going to stay here with you."

His pronouncement struck her like a punch to the gut, creating an ache between her ribs. "Absolutely not."

Having him there in her space, night after night, would make it much more difficult to remember the makeshift boundary she'd created to protect herself between Rhys the FBI agent and Rhys the ordinary man. Even now, she wanted nothing more than for him to wrap his arms around her and kiss away her fears. In some ways, Rhys was even more dangerous to her than the Composer.

HUNTING A HOMETOWN KILLER

SHELLY BELL

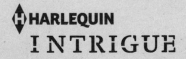

To Jason, Kylie and Spencer. Thank you for helping me find
new ways to kill a person. I couldn't ask for a better family.

H HARLEQUIN®
INTRIGUE™

Recycling programs
for this product may
not exist in your area.

ISBN-13: 978-1-335-58275-1

Hunting a Hometown Killer

Copyright © 2023 by Shelly Bell

For questions and comments about the quality of this book,
please contact us at CustomerService@Harlequin.com.

Harlequin Enterprises ULC
22 Adelaide St. West, 41st Floor
Toronto, Ontario M5H 4E3, Canada
www.Harlequin.com

Printed in U.S.A.

Shelly Bell is the author of more than a dozen romances. Her novels have collected numerous awards and have received starred reviews from both *Publishers Weekly* and *Library Journal*. An attorney for more than twenty-five years, Shelly lives with her family in southwest Florida. To learn more about her books, visit www.ShellyBellBooks.com.

Books by Shelly Bell

Harlequin Intrigue

Shield of Honor

Hunting a Hometown Killer

Visit the Author Profile page at Harlequin.com.

CAST OF CHARACTERS

Rhys Keller—This FBI special agent refuses to lose another victim to the serial killer known as the Composer, especially not the only woman he's ever loved.

Julia Harcourt—The world-renowned violinist's return to Laurel Creek has caught the dangerous attention of the Composer.

Sam Keller—Rhys's twin brother and a special agent for the investigative service branch of the National Park Service.

Joshua Keller—Rhys's older brother and Division Commander of the Laurel Creek Sheriff Department's Criminal Investigations.

Griffin Keller—Rhys's father and previous Laurel Creek sheriff.

Alicia Keller—Rhys's mother, murdered when he was a child.

Daniel Fenske—Conductor of the Laurel Creek Symphony and father figure to Julia.

Owen Baker—A janitor at the symphony when Julia was a teenager and boyfriend of a Composer victim.

Lewis Vogel—Julia's teenage rival and current second-chair violinist at the symphony.

William Pearce—Laurel Creek sheriff.

Chapter One

With its fragrant forests of pines and oaks, the Blue Ridge Mountains had always been FBI Special Agent Rhys Keller's refuge from reality. Growing up in the nearby town of Laurel Creek, he'd hiked the Chattahoochee-Oconee National Forest's trails hundreds of times. He'd fished in its cool streams and climbed the mountain's summit. Camped there with his brothers when things had gotten too rough at home.

But today, his fond childhood memories of the forest had been tainted by violence. Even the fresh Georgia air couldn't mask the scent of death as he watched the local coroner's vehicle drive away with the female victim's body inside.

Parched from the summer heat, he tipped back his full bottle of water and drank it dry. The sun was setting behind jagged rocks, casting a long shadow on the trail's entrance. Gone from the gravel parking lot were the news vans and law enforcement vehicles. Only two cars remained, one being his, but he couldn't get himself to leave.

After working for fifteen hours straight, Rhys should be exhausted, ready to drop after riding high on a day's worth of adrenaline surges. Instead, he was more determined than ever to find the monster behind the string of murders.

Because of Rhys's failure, another parent had lost their daughter.

Her death rested squarely on his shoulders.

Hearing footsteps coming from behind him, Rhys didn't have to look to know it was his twin. As a special agent in the ISB, the investigative service branch of the National Park Service, Sam had been assigned to the case last month upon the discovery of the first victim on the Appalachian National Scenic Trail. It wasn't until a few days later, when a second victim was found on the Appalachian Trail, that the FBI and Rhys had gotten involved.

"I know what you're thinking," Sam said, stopping beside him, "and it's not your fault. There's nothing you could have done."

"You're wrong. I might not have killed her, but it's because of me that she died." As lead on the case, the primary responsibility for the investigation fell on his shoulders and no one else's. Although the forensics team had finished processing the crime scene an hour ago, a short piece of yellow crime scene tape still clung to the trail's welcome sign. He snatched the tape and shoved it in the bear-proof trash can. "If

I did my job, he wouldn't have had the opportunity to take another life."

The bodies of Jessica Sanchez, Leanne Topper and Emma Ginsberg had all been found somewhere along the Appalachian Trail within twenty-four hours of going missing and all within the last month. The first two, Jessica and Leanne, had been kidnapped in their apartment parking lots, their purses and keys left behind near their cars. Emma had been abducted while tossing out the trash at the diner where she worked.

Three male hikers on summer break from college had discovered the most recent victim this morning at six. By the time Rhys had driven the hour and a half from his apartment in Atlanta to the crime scene, the news about the murder had hit the airwaves. To Rhys's dismay, the media had begun calling the serial killer the Composer for his signature of tattooing music stanzas on the victims' backs.

Someone had not only disclosed the details about the newest victim, they'd also supplied photos of the tattoo to the media. He'd wager it had been one of the hikers who'd found her. Since this morning, the FBI had logged hundreds of calls from people claiming to know the origins of the tattoo, making it more complicated to filter out the credible tips.

"If you did your job..." Sam took off his hat and wiped his brow. "Rhys, that's all you do. When was the last time you took a day off? Heck, when was the last time you slept more than four hours?"

"Don't you have something else to do other than lecture your twin?" Rhys didn't need it. Not now, when every moment counted. There had to be something they'd missed, something that would provide a clue as to how to find the Composer before he could kill again.

He turned and headed back to where they'd found the body, kicking up a cloud of dirt as his boots hit the narrow trail.

Night descended as the tall hardwoods blocked the last of the sun's rays. The air remained humid, the moisture so thick he could practically taste it on his tongue. He wasn't sure what he expected to find out here in the dark, but he refused to leave without a lead.

"No. Not really," Sam said, following behind Rhys like the younger brother he was—albeit only by six minutes. "You know what happens when you let a case consume you."

Rhys should have known his brother wouldn't leave it alone. If there was one thing Rhys could count on, it was Sam's determination. Something all three of the Keller brothers had in common. "This isn't the same. I'm not Dad."

"Not yet, but it's a slippery slope. You missed dinner again."

No matter what was going on in his brothers' lives or how busy they got, they still had Sabbath dinner together every Friday night at their childhood home.

It had begun when they'd been kids as a way to honor their mother's memory.

Later, it had become a way for them to make sure none of them turned into their father, a shell of a man obsessed by an unsolved case.

Rhys had missed the last four.

That didn't make him their father. Even though the Sabbath dinners had been held in his dining room for the last twenty years, he'd missed almost all of them, too lost in his memories to appreciate the family he had left.

"I'm fine," Rhys said. "Give it a rest."

Sam met Rhys stride for stride down the narrow trail. "If you don't slow down, you're going to burn out like he did."

It didn't matter if Rhys did burn out. Unlike his father, he didn't have three motherless boys to raise. He had no one waiting for him at home, no one relying on him but the victims' families and the Composer's potential targets. He owed it to them to give everything he had to give, and if that meant he suffered a few sleepless nights and skipped a few meals, so be it.

"I'll slow down when I catch the Composer." Rhys pushed a low-hanging branch out of the way, the rough scrape of it slicing his palm. He shook off the sting and didn't bother checking to see if he was bleeding. Whatever pain he felt was nothing compared to what the Composer's victims had endured.

Sam grabbed Rhys's arm, forcing him to stop.

"There's always going to be one more serial killer for you to chase."

Rhys shook off his brother's hold. "Not in our hometown."

This case was different. Any one of the victims could have been someone they'd grown up with. Someone like—

He couldn't go there.

It was a coincidence that all the Composer's victims were blonde and in their late twenties to early thirties.

Besides, Julia Harcourt hadn't lived in Georgia for twelve years. As far as he knew, she was safe and sound in Europe. Still, ever since he'd gotten assigned to this case, he'd been having the same recurring nightmare he'd experienced during his teen years of that woman drowning in a lake.

"I get it," Sam said. "It's as if these murders are happening in our own backyard. But you need to remain objective and treat this case like any other. Else, you'll fall down the same dark well that Dad fell into after Mom was murdered."

No matter how much Rhys worked, he'd never lose himself in a case as thoroughly as his father had done. Twenty years later and his dad was just as obsessed with finding his wife's killer as the day it had happened. His love for her had damned him to a prison of his own making.

Since Rhys had no plans of ever falling in love again, there would be no chance for him to repeat his father's mistakes. "Fine. I promise I'll be at Dad's next Friday night. I'll even man the grill."

Sam remained quiet, his gaze assessing. Whatever Sam saw on Rhys's face must have convinced him to let the issue go.

Now in complete darkness, they each switched on their flashlights, providing enough illumination to avoid tripping on any of the trail's unexpected rocks or getting whacked by another branch.

Ferns and wildflowers blanketed the ground on both sides of the trail, creating the perfect hiding spots for the small animals that lived in the lush forest. As Rhys and Sam hiked farther into the wilderness, nearby creatures scurried in their natural habitat, snapping twigs and rustling bushes. From only two miles away, Rhys could hear the waterfall spilling into the stream.

Without the hum of people and flurry of activity to distract him, memories from that fateful day twelve years ago crashed into him. It was the last time he'd felt that waterfall's cool mist on his skin... and the last time he'd felt Julia Harcourt's lush lips on his.

He'd spent that afternoon on the bank of the stream, lying on a blanket with their limbs intertwined and her head on his chest as she spoke about a future he knew would never come. Even now, he could still recall sifting his fingers through the softness of her hair and the hate in her eyes later than night when he'd broken up with her.

"I heard back from the backpack manufacturer," Sam said, piercing the silence with his voice and jarring Rhys back to the present. "The one our killer uses to carry his victims to the dump site is its most popular model. Over a hundred thousand of them have been sold over the last few years."

Rhys swore under his breath.

Evidence had suggested the Composer tattooed and murdered his victims elsewhere before leaving their bodies in the park. A small scrap of blood-soaked fabric snagged by a mossy rock was found near Leanne's body. Forensics identified it as the kind used in waterproof backpacks. It explained why the victims' bodies had been curled in the fetal position, with their knees tucked and their arms folded over their chests. Worn on his back, he'd carried them that way to transport their bodies into the park without capturing anyone's attention. Although the carbon fiber backpack's frame made it possible to carry the weight load by distributing it across his hips, back and shoulders, the killer still had to be strong enough to accomplish it.

Even knowing it was a long shot, Rhys had hoped the fabric would provide him with a list of possible suspects. The killer could be almost anyone.

The FBI's behavioral analysts had created a profile of their suspect based on the evidence so far. They knew the Composer was likely male, intelligent and able to blend in. Since the victims were all discovered within a hundred-mile radius of each other in North Georgia, he had to live somewhere nearby.

Rhys's stomach churned from the knowledge that unless he arrested the killer in the next few days, another woman would go missing.

Approaching the crime scene, Sam aimed his flashlight on the spot where the victim had been found. "What is it you're hoping to find?"

"I don't know. A miracle, maybe?" Rhys dropped to his knees and swept his fingers over the trail's dirt as if it held all the answers. With the light in his hand, he lay flat on his stomach to get a different view of the area.

What was it about the Appalachian Trail that appealed to the killer? If he wanted his victims discovered quickly, certainly there were more convenient places to leave them. Why here and why now? And why tattoo the women before killing them?

The FBI's Behavioral Analysis Unit, or BAU, boasted the top forensic psychologists in the world. They theorized the tattoo was the Composer's signature, meaning it had originated from the killer's fantasies, and that while other details might evolve as the Composer continued killing, the signature would never change. Getting into the mind of a serial killer wasn't as easy as they made it out on television. A profile was a tool, but it wasn't a road map.

Intermingled with the walnut-colored soil, a dark red sediment caught Rhys's eye. Donning a plastic glove, he stretched out his arm for a sample, rubbing the claylike substance between his thumb and forefinger. This iron-rich soil wasn't typically found on this trail.

Soil contained identifying markers that could be traced to a specific location.

"Hey, Sam? I think I got something." Rhys pulled out an evidence tube from his pants' pocket and collected the soil for analysis. They'd already taken several samples from where the victim had rested, as well as the area surrounding her body, but this one was farther away.

Plenty of law enforcement officers had plodded over this area today. While they should've been wearing booties over their shoes, any one of them could have inadvertently tainted the scene. Or, more likely, it had been deposited by a hiker's shoes prior to the murder.

At any rate, it was something that didn't belong.

Jumping to his feet, Rhys dropped the tube back into his pocket, snapped off his glove. He flipped toward Sam, who flinched as the flashlight's beam hit his face. "Ever see any—"

A snapping of twigs and an unmistakable human gasp came from behind him.

Rhys spun around and scanned the area with his flashlight.

The trail was empty.

But he hadn't imagined the gasp. Ten years of law enforcement experience and the expression on his brother's face told him that.

Someone was hiding nearby in the woods.

Nodding to Sam in a silent signal, they both retrieved their guns from their holsters and stalked closer to where the noise had originated. "FBI! Identify yourself!"

Except for the faint rumble of the waterfall and the distant chirping of grasshoppers, it remained eerily quiet. Rhys's gut burned with foreboding. It wasn't unusual for serial killers to return to the scene, either to watch law enforcement work or to relive the murder. Was it possible that the Composer was here, hiding in the woods?

Rhys didn't take a breath as he waited for the unknown interloper to make his move.

From thirty feet away, a dark figure jumped out from behind a tree and bolted toward the park entrance.

"Call it in," Rhys shouted at Sam as he chased after the runner. "FBI! Freeze!" His adrenaline spiked, giving him an extra shot of energy.

Wearing a long black jacket with a hood over his head, the stranger was about a foot shorter and not nearly as fast as Rhys. It didn't take much for Rhys to eat the distance between them. Reaching out, he nabbed the back of the guy's jacket and crashed into him.

As they tumbled to the ground, Rhys flipped the man over and tugged back the hood of the jacket. Long blond hair spilled out.

Stunned, Rhys pinned the body beneath him with

his own. The most beautiful blue eyes he'd ever encountered stared up at him from a heart-shaped face.

He didn't need his flashlight to know those eyes
were the same color blue as the Georgia sky on a
cloudless summer day or that the hair felt like silk
in the palm of his hand.

It had been twelve years, but their bodies still
fit together as if they were made for one another.
"Julia?"

Chapter Two

A breathless Julia gave him a half-hearted smile. "Hello, Rhys."

The fact that she couldn't breathe had nothing to do with her short run and everything to do with the man currently lying on top of her. Rhys Keller hadn't just broken her heart when he'd ended their relationship twelve years ago.

He'd pulverized it.

For a moment, Rhys just stared at her as if he couldn't believe his eyes. She understood the feeling. "What were you thinking being alone out here with a killer on the loose?" he sputtered. "Are you insane? You can't be here, Julia. This is a crime scene."

Indignation filled her. It wasn't as if she wanted to be there. "I'm not alone now, am I? You're here."

His voice went low, its timbre vibrating through her body. "You came for me?"

How foolish she'd been at eighteen, believing the two of them belonged together. She'd convinced herself they'd get married after high school and attend the local university together. That he'd work for the sheriff and she'd become a music teacher.

Rhys had shattered that illusion into a million jagged little pieces when he'd told her he'd never loved her.

And never would.

"No," she said, swallowing down the lump in her throat. "I had no idea you'd be here." That was the truth. Had she known he'd be on this particular trail, she would have found a different way to get in touch with the FBI.

She wished she could say the years had healed her broken heart, but the sad truth was, seeing him there, in the place where they'd spent their last day together, brought the pain back to the surface.

In some ways, it was as if no time had passed at all. He even smelled the same, that mouthwatering combination of cedarwood soap and his own natural musk. If she closed her eyes, she could almost believe they were back in high school, when nothing was more complicated than passing physics.

But her blue eyes remained wide open.

Approaching footsteps pounded on the dirt, reminding her they weren't alone. "Rhys! Did you…?" Sam stopped, the beam from his flashlight on her and Rhys. "Julia?"

"False alarm, Sam," Rhys said, without taking his gaze off her face.

Sam chuckled. "Yeah, I see that."

She suddenly became conscious of Rhys's body

pressed against hers and the pebbles underneath poking into her thighs. "Could you let me up please? You're a lot heavier than you were when you were eighteen."

"Sorry." Rhys lifted himself off her and stood. "But in all fairness, I wouldn't have chased after you if you hadn't run."

If that was true, then why had he let her leave for Europe without so much as a goodbye?

Wrapping his fingers around her wrist, Rhys yanked her to her feet as if she weighed no more than a feather. He held on to her wrist far longer than necessary. When he let go, he scooped up his flashlight and holstered his pistol.

"Been a long time, Julia," Sam said.

Even though Sam and Rhys were identical twins, she'd always been able to tell them apart. Sam had a small scar underneath his eye from where a three-year-old Rhys had accidentally cut him while shaving Sam with one of their father's razors. But the major difference between them reflected in their eyes. Sam's were full of cynicism and wariness while Rhys's were more accepting and trusting. It was what drew her to Rhys that first sunny day when the Keller boys brought cookies to her house as a welcome to the community.

"It has." She rubbed her thumb over the skin where Rhys had touched.

Throughout high school, the Keller brothers had been like family. The guardian her parents had hired had made it clear she wasn't there to be Julia's friend. She'd cleaned, cooked and driven Julia to rehearsals, but that had been the extent of their relationship. That's why Julia had spent all of her free time at the Keller house. When Rhys and she had broken up, she'd lost more than a boyfriend. She'd lost them all.

Sam's gaze bounced between Rhys and Julia. "Why don't I give you two some privacy?"

"Before you go—" Rhys handed Sam a tube "—have the lab see if they can determine the soil's origin."

"Will do. And I'll cancel the backup." Sam grinned. "Good to see you, Julia."

As soon as Sam disappeared from view, Rhys began the inevitable interrogation. "Mind telling me why you ran from me when I identified myself as FBI?"

"I don't know. I guess… I saw Sam's face and heard your voice, and I just panicked." She'd seen the vehicles in the lot and walked up the path, never thinking for one second she'd find Rhys at the end of it. "I didn't realize… I didn't know you and Sam worked for the FBI."

"Just me. Sam's a special agent in the ISB, the National Park Service's investigative department," Rhys said.

It didn't surprise Julia that Sam had gone to work for the national parks. When they'd been younger, he'd spent all his free time outside, hiking and fishing in the summer and skiing and snowboarding in the winter. But she was surprised Rhys had joined the FBI. He and his older brother Joshua had always been intent on joining the sheriff's office and staying in Laurel Creek. Sam might be Rhys's twin, but Joshua had been his idol.

Boiling in the humid air, Julia undid the first two buttons of her trench coat. She'd come to the park straight from work, and since a skirt and blouse weren't conducive for a walk in the park, she'd thrown on the jacket. "I called the FBI hotline this morning, but no one called me back. When I finished work, I thought I'd drive here and see if I could speak to the agent in charge of the Composer case."

He shifted his weight from one leg to the other. "That would be me."

"Oh." She should've seen this coming. Rhys didn't just work for the FBI. He was the person she'd come here for. She was kicking herself for not inquiring about Rhys when she'd last spoken to Joshua. "Well, I guess my plan worked."

"Let's start from the beginning. Why do you need to talk to the FBI about the Composer case?"

"This morning when I was getting ready for work, I saw the news report about the woman who was found here. They flashed a photograph of the tattoo." Just thinking about the picture nauseated her. "I recognized the music."

He frowned. "The FBI searched all published music for a match. We didn't find one."

"That's because it's not published yet. I wrote it." She squared her shoulders, proud of her achievements and yet disgusted that someone had warped her art for their own evil purpose.

"Who have you shared it with? Who knows about it?"

"I haven't shared that particular piece with anyone, but thousands of people around the world are aware I've been composing. It's not as if it's a well-kept secret." Was it wrong to be disappointed that he hadn't kept up with her career? "In the last two years, I've spent less time touring and more time composing. I grew tired of living out of suitcases and having my schedule planned out for months at a time. I wanted a normal life. I took a position at the Laurel Creek Symphony."

Rhys stepped closer, towering over her. "You moved back? What about Europe?"

"I loved Europe—the people, the culture, the food. I even bought myself an apartment in Paris overlooking the Seine. But I barely got the chance to spend any time there. And it wasn't home."

The house she'd moved into at the end of eighth grade in Laurel Creek had been the closest she'd ever gotten. Before that, she'd never stayed in one place for more than a few months. Her parents, famous musicians who guest-accompanied symphonies all over the world, had brought her with them, hiring tutors to teach her rather than sending her to school. Mornings were spent studying math and science, and afternoons were scheduled for practicing violin. Her friends had been the children of other musicians, but her friendships never lasted long. Not until she'd convinced her parents to allow her to attend high school in the States and they'd bought the house in Laurel Creek, Georgia.

Not until she'd met the Keller boys.

Rhys waved his hand toward the path, and they both began walking toward the direction of the parking lot. "So, how did the Composer get his hands on the piece?"

Despite it being hot as Hades outside and her wearing a jacket, she shivered. She'd asked herself the same question all day, and there was only one reasonable answer. "It was stolen from my house."

His lips pressed together in a flat line. "When?"

"About a month ago, just a few days after I moved back. I'd been working, tweaking the ending on the piece before I went to rehearsal, and when I came home, it was gone." Since she composed using online music notation software, it was only a printed copy of the composition. The original remained on her computer.

It had creeped her out to know someone had managed to invade the place meant to keep her safe. She felt as if she'd been violated. But what happened to her wasn't anything compared to those poor dead girls.

"Where are you living?" he asked.

"The same house I lived in before. The one down the road from yours." A mile of dense woods separated their two houses. How many times had she cut through the forest to get to the Keller house? She could still recall the fluttering of excitement she experienced whenever she followed the creek to the Kellers' backyard and found Rhys there waiting for her.

"I thought your parents sold it when you left." He scratched his cheek over a bit of dark stubble. That was new. At eighteen, he'd yet to grow any facial hair. "There was a nice older couple who lived there."

"The Coopers. They just leased it."

Her parents had intended to sell, but she'd pleaded with them to rent it out as an investment. Then, a couple years after she'd moved to Europe, she'd bought it from them.

"Other than the composition, what else was taken?"

She stumbled, losing balance as the path made a sudden dip. Rhys steadied her, wrapping his arm around her waist. She froze and swallowed the lump in her throat. In another time and place, she might have mistaken his behavior as intimate. But she wasn't a fool. Rhys was just doing his job. She was a possible witness in his murder case. That was all.

On a nod of silent thanks, she pulled away from him, and they continued to stroll toward the trail's exit. "Nothing else was missing. I know it sounds weird, but I could tell whoever broke in touched my things. It was just little things like a wrinkle in the blanket on my bed, and my underwear drawer was slightly open."

He remained quiet until they reached the gravel of

the parking lot. The nearby streetlamps cast enough light to give Julia her first good look at Rhys in twelve years.

The structure of his face hadn't changed. All the Keller boys had been blessed with high cheekbones, wide foreheads, straight noses and narrow chins. What was different now were the subtle lines bracketing the corners of his mouth and the scruff that hid his dimples. Also, he wore his russet hair much shorter now, closer to his scalp rather than the floppy locks that had been all the rage back then.

Those weren't the only changes. He'd definitely filled out, his shoulders and chest much broader and his legs more solid. She'd felt the added weight of him when he'd been lying on top of her, but until now, she hadn't understood the extent of his transformation. He was no longer the boy she'd known.

Now, he was very much a man.

Rhys's tired hazel eyes examined her with intensity. Did he see the changes in her?

He hooked his hands in his pockets and rocked back on his heels. "Are you certain you didn't misplace the composition? Maybe took it to rehearsal and left it there?"

"Yes, I'm sure." She shoved down the hurt that while she'd been stupidly admiring his physique, he'd been questioning her story about the burglary. "You don't believe me, do you?" She turned from him. "The sheriff's office didn't either. They didn't come out and say it, but they didn't do anything to investigate. Just took my statement and said they'd look into it. They didn't even dust for prints."

"Hey," Rhys said softly, placing his hand on her shoulder. He rotated her toward him and leaned down, his face solemn. "If you say someone broke in and stole the composition, I believe you."

She couldn't stop herself from reaching out and touching him. It was as if her fingers had a mind of their own, sweeping across the ridge of his cheek. He was so warm, so real. Behind the laugh lines and the whiskers was the same boy she'd always known, the one who'd sat in the front row at all of her recitals, shown her how to climb a tree and taught her the prayer when lighting the Sabbath candles. Rhys had given Julia her first true taste of what it was like to have a family.

Before he'd snatched it all away from her in an instant.

Rhys walked Julia to her silver four-door SUV. "Do you have anyone watching over you? A husband maybe?"

Not bothering to look at him, she clicked the key fob, unlocking the car's doors. "That's none of your business." What did he care? It was obvious he hadn't checked on her in all these years.

"Seeing as I'm the special agent in charge of the Composer investigation, your safety is one hundred percent my business," he said, reminding her, once again, that the only reason they were talking was because she was a witness in his murder investigation.

They stopped beside her SUV. "Listen, I don't like the thought of you alone in that house. Maybe you could stay at a hotel for the time being. Or even better—" head down, he kicked the gravel with the tip of his shoe "—go back to Europe until I find this guy."

Irritation heating her from the inside, she yanked off her jacket and tossed it into her vehicle. She may have walked away twelve years ago without a fight, but she wasn't going to do it again. "You have some nerve using your case as an excuse to get rid of me. I've moved back to Laurel Creek, and I'm staying, whether you like it or not. I won't allow anyone— and that includes you—to kick me out of my home."

He blew out a breath and ran his hand over his scalp. "I didn't mean it like that. Your house is se-cluded, and someone   likely the man responsible for four murders—already got inside of it once. It would be reckless of me as an officer of the law not to request you stay elsewhere. And as your friend, I want you as far away from this nightmare as possi-ble. But you're right. I shouldn't have suggested you leave the country. That was out of line. I apologize."

It was difficult to stay mad at him when he seemed so contrite, even though a petty part of her wanted to. "I accept your apology."

"At least let me follow you home to make sure you get in safely."

She shook her head as she slid into the driver's seat. "I'll be fine."

"One second." Rhys took out a card from his wallet and wrote on the back of it. "Here's my card. I wrote my cell number on it. Make sure to text me when you get home."

In those final moments, she memorized his face, every wrinkle and every fleck of gold in his irises, realizing it may be the last time she'd ever see it. "Goodbye, Rhys."

She drove away and didn't look back once. It was a marked improvement over the last time they'd said goodbye, when she'd remained hopeful until the last moment that he would change his mind. Now, she knew better.

Maybe she should have taken him up on his offer to follow her home, but she was just so tired of everyone telling her what to do and how to do it. First her parents and then the legal guardian they'd employed to act in their absence. As a child, she'd had no choice, but she'd promised herself that the day she became an adult, she would break free from her parents' constraints. Yet when Rhys had ended their relationship, all she had wanted to do was run from her heartbreak. And she'd kept running for years until one day, she'd realized she'd broken the promise to herself.

No one would take her independence from her again. She knew Rhys meant well. As protective as he was when it came to those he cared about, he'd never once treated Julia as if she were helpless or weak.

But she couldn't rely on him to protect her anymore. Those days were over.

She would and could take care of herself.

In the first few days following the burglary, she'd been on edge, worried whoever had stolen the composition would return. She'd gotten her locks changed, had added motion sensor lights outside and had hired a service to fix the alarm. After that, she'd been so busy with rehearsals, she'd stuck the burglary into the back of her mind. Until this morning, she'd had little reason to be concerned.

After a ten-minute drive, she turned onto her home's long dark driveway. An allée of oak trees arched over the drive's pebbled pavement. Before tonight, she'd appreciated the property's solitude, but now, on high alert, she scanned her surroundings as if danger lurked behind every tree.

It had unnerved her to hear the Composer had killed again, but seeing the photograph of her music tattooed on the victim's back had struck Julia with utter terror. Why would someone do such a thing? And why use Julia's music to do it?

Julia parked on the circular drive in front of her house and popped the liftgate. While the unsettled part of her wanted to run inside as quickly as possible, she would never leave her violin in her vehicle overnight. Hand-carved and custom-made for her by a friend of her father, the instrument was her most cherished possession. She'd been relieved she'd taken it with her the day of the burglary. Now in light of the murders, it seemed like such a selfish thing to worry about.

She walked to the back of her vehicle and retrieved her instrument. Holding the case, she reached up with her free hand to shut the liftgate.

Without warning, something yanked her backward, the brutal force of it causing her to drop her violin to the ground. *What was happening?* Fear froze her limbs and scattered her thoughts. *Where had he come from?*

Would she be the Composer's next victim?

Her heartbeat thundered in her ears. Before she could shout for help, a leather-gloved hand covered her mouth.

Her cries wouldn't have mattered anyway.

There was no one around to hear them.

Chapter Three

In no mood for distractions, Rhys flicked off the car's radio.

His stomach churned at the idea of Julia caught up in some psychopath's web. He didn't believe much in coincidences. Hadn't he himself noticed the physical similarities between all the victims and Julia? He'd chalked it up to being in the park where they'd spent their last day together, but now, he knew better.

When Sam had first brought the FBI into the case, Rhys had run the crime through ViCAP, the Violent Criminal Apprehension Program, a national database that analyzed unsolved crimes to find similarities. It was possible the killer's modus operandi, commonly referred to as an MO, had evolved over time, but the ViCAP hadn't come up with any hits. That meant the murders had begun shortly after Julia's return to Georgia.

He didn't want to jump to conclusions, but it almost seemed as if Julia had been the *catalyst* for the murders. What was the connection between Julia and the Composer?

If he had his way, Julia's life would never be tainted by violence or terror. He and his brothers had been young when they'd come home from school and found their mother's lifeless body on the dining room floor. The experience had shaped them all into the men they were today. They understood that once evil had touched them, it would follow them the rest of their lives, and they had a duty to fight it.

Rhys had wanted to shield Julia from his world and had done what he'd needed to do in order to achieve it. He'd *lied* to her. Convinced her they had no future together. It had been the only way to persuade her to leave Laurel Creek and keep her safe. But it had all been done in vain. Despite Rhys's best efforts, violence had found Julia anyway.

That's why he hadn't listened to her when she'd insisted he not follow her home. He'd hung back to prevent her from spotting him, but he'd kept her SUV in his sights until the car in front of him had stopped at a yellow light, causing Rhys to lose her.

He tapped his fingers on the steering wheel as he passed his childhood home. While Julia's house was set farther back, his father's dwelling was close to the road. Rhys eyed Joshua's patrol car parked beside their dad's black pickup truck. As division commander of the sheriff's department's Criminal Investigations Division, Joshua lived in an apartment not too far from there and tried to stop by at the end of every shift to make sure their dad ate dinner and took his heart medication.

Rhys's neck prickled from his unease. He jammed his foot harder on the accelerator as he made his way up Julia's driveway.

As soon as his car cleared the trees, Rhys saw, to his horror, that his intuition had been correct.

A man with a dark ski mask held Julia captive, restraining her with his arms. Wiggling and twisting her body, Julia struggled to break free.

Rhys threw his car into Park and jumped out, raising his Glock. From Rhys's vantage point, he didn't see a weapon in the suspect's hands, but that didn't mean he didn't have one.

It took all of his training to portray an outward appearance of calm and control, while inside, he was anything but. "FBI! Let the woman go and put your hands up!"

Julia's attacker whipped his head over his shoulder to look at Rhys. Using the distraction, Julia elbowed him hard in the gut and kicked her leg backward, ramming her foot into his knee. The man groaned as his leg buckled, and he lost his balance. Julia used her full weight to shove him backward and break out of his hold. She ran away, providing Rhys with unencumbered access to her attacker.

For a split second, Rhys considered shooting. His grip tightened on the butt of his gun. He'd be doing the world a favor. The man had possibly murdered four women and would have taken Julia. No one would mourn a serial killer.

Then rational thought jerked him back to reality. As much as he wanted the man dead for daring to even touch Julia, Rhys had no justification for it.

He moved toward the suspect to take him into custody. "You're under arrest for the attempted kidnapping of Julia Harcourt."

The man took off, hurdling into the trees and disappearing into the darkness. Rhys couldn't let him get away. He sprinted after him. No one knew those woods better than Rhys.

"Rhys! Stay with me," Julia cried from behind him. "Please."

With one foot on the grass and another in the forest, Rhys froze, his mind torn between two opposing needs. If he didn't capture the suspect, he was potentially putting lives at risk. But he couldn't leave Julia alone. What if the suspect returned while Rhys was out there looking for him?

He holstered his gun and strode to Julia. "Are you all right? He didn't hurt you?" He gathered her into his arms, tucking her under his chin and feeling her tremble against him.

"I'm fine. He just scared me," she said. "He came out of nowhere and grabbed me from behind." She released a shuttered breath, the puff of air warm against the skin of his neck. All too soon, she stepped back, a black leather glove dangling from her fingers. "This was his. Also, I scratched his hand when I pulled it off him."

Rhys grabbed the glove. Hope swelled in his chest

like a balloon. Julia's attacker might have left DNA inside the glove or under her fingernails. If the guy had committed prior offenses, it was possible his DNA was already in CODIS, the Combined DNA Index System.

Julia hurried to her instrument. "Oh, my violin." Kneeling on the pavement, she unlatched the case. "Thank goodness." She lifted her violin and flipped it from side to side, examining it.

Only Julia would worry more about her violin than herself.

"I'm calling Joshua." He dialed his brother's cell and put his phone on speaker. When his brother answered, he skipped the formalities. "Joshua. I'm at Julia's house. Someone just attacked her."

"I'll be right over," Joshua said before immediately hanging up.

Rhys studied Julia as she lovingly placed her violin back into its case. "Joshua didn't ask me any questions. He already knew you moved back, didn't he?"

She stood holding the case close to her side. "Yes. He was one of the officers who responded to the call about the burglary. I told him not to tell you."

Fighting the urge to curse out his brother, Rhys clenched his jaw. Joshua should have mentioned it to him. Then maybe he wouldn't have been so blindsided to see her tonight. He might have spoken to her about the burglary and connected it to his case—maybe prevented the murders. Resting a hand on the small of Julia's spine, Rhys led her to her front porch.

As they waited for Joshua, Rhys grabbed a kit from the trunk of his car and clipped her fingernails for possible cells left behind by her attacker. But it was more likely to find DNA inside the glove.

It wasn't the biggest or fanciest home in Laurel Creek, but it was as unique as the woman who owned it. The house was circular rather than angular, with a wraparound porch and large picture windows that provided full views of the surrounding forests and the distant mountain tops. One of his fondest memories was of he and Julia sitting on the glider porch swing, holding hands while watching the fireworks explode above the mountains on the Fourth of July.

"What are you doing here?" she asked, perching on the top step of the porch stairs. She set the violin behind her and patted the space beside her. "I told you I didn't need you to follow me home." She put on a brave front, but her hands were shaking. The attack had rattled her.

He sat beside her. "Obviously, I didn't listen, and it's a good thing too." If he'd arrived a minute later, he might have been too late. He didn't want to think about what could have happened to her.

"Thank you. I appreciate you helping me, but I'm fine now. I'll go inside, lock the door and wait for Joshua. You don't need to stay."

The quiver in her voice betrayed her. She might not want to, but she did, in fact, need him.

Headlights shone on them as a vehicle approached. Squinting, Rhys stood, just able to make out the shape of the approaching sheriff's car and the figure behind the wheel. "That's not Josh."

Sheriff William Pearce got out of the car, leaving his engine running. He sauntered up to the house as if he had all the time in the world. "Rhys."

How had the sheriff learned about the attack on Julia?

And how had he gotten here so quickly?

He'd arrived before Joshua, who was only a mile away.

Rhys shoved the glove into his pocket and stepped off the porch. "Sheriff. Surprised to see you."

Although Pearce was around the same age as Rhys's father, he looked about twenty years younger, no doubt the result of a healthier lifestyle. Shorter than Rhys's six feet by a couple inches, with a mustache and neatly trimmed goatee, Sheriff Pearce had worked under Rhys's father when he'd been sheriff. They'd never gotten along, although Rhys's father claimed Pearce was a decent cop. It had more to do with the way they approached policing.

Sheriff Pearce had always been more political, concerned with schmoozing the right sort of people in order to get and then stay in power. There'd been rumors Pearce had an eye on running for governor one day. Rhys's dad had stayed out of politics as much as possible. He'd focused on keeping the community safe from crime and figured if he did a good job, he'd get reelected. He'd been successful too, until the day his wife had been murdered.

A car made its way up Julia's driveway and parked beside Sheriff Pearce's. Joshua ran toward them, his brows arched in confusion. Rhys would bet his brother was wondering how the sheriff had beaten him there. As he got closer, Joshua shook his head at Rhys in warning. He knew how Rhys felt about his father's replacement.

Pearce hooked his thumbs in his pants' pockets. "I was on my way home when Captain Keller called it in," he said, referring to Joshua. "Since I was nearby, I thought I'd personally come by to make sure Ms. Harcourt was all right." He jutted his chin toward Julia. "There was an attempted abduction, you said?"

"Yes. It happened so fast," Julia said, joining them at the edge of the drive. "He came up from behind me and put his hand over my mouth."

"Any weapon?" Joshua asked, pen and paper in hand to take the report.

Julia frowned. "I don't know."

"Not that I saw," Rhys offered.

The sheriff's gaze darted between Rhys and Julia before resting on Rhys. "You were there?"

"I followed Ms. Harcourt home," Rhys explained. "I was less than a minute behind her. She was struggling to break free from the suspect when I arrived."

"And then?" Sheriff Pearce asked.

Rhys watched his brother, wondering why he'd relegated himself to silent note taker.

"He and I fought. He ran off," Julia said.

"What did *you* do?" Pearce didn't even try to hide the judgment from his voice.

Rhys didn't understand why the sheriff wasn't taking the attack more seriously. Had the man forgotten there was a killer on the loose? Or was this his way of sulking because his office hadn't played a bigger role in the latest victim's murder investigation? While the Jane Doe had been found in Laurel Creek's city limits, the National Park Service had jurisdiction over the case, and they'd already brought in the FBI. It was Rhys's job to coordinate all the different departments so that nothing fell through the cracks. If Sheriff Pearce didn't approve, that was his problem, but Rhys had no time to play politics.

Rhys folded his arms across his chest, sensing where the sheriff was going with the line of questioning and not liking it. "I stayed with Ms. Harcourt."

"You just let the suspect get away? Why didn't you go after him?" Pearce asked accusingly.

Julia wrapped a hand around Rhys's biceps. "I asked him not to."

Sheriff Pearce smirked as if he knew a secret. "Right, of course you did."

Rhys couldn't take much more of Pearce's disrespect. He needed to speak to the man alone. "Joshua, could you take Julia inside and finish taking her statement? I'd like a word with Sheriff Pearce."

The sheriff nodded at Joshua, giving him permission to leave.

Once Julia and Joshua were safely out of earshot, Rhys cut to the chase. "Stop with the passive-aggressive interrogation, Sheriff. What exactly are you trying to insinuate?"

"I'm not insinuating anything." Pearce stroked his beard. "But you must admit, it seems awfully convenient. You happen to get here where she's attacked by someone with no weapon, and then she prevents you from apprehending him. You do the math."

Rhys didn't understand what Sheriff Pearce had against Julia. "What, you think she set it up? To what end?"

"Julia Harcourt has always been a lonely girl, hasn't she?"

Rhys clenched and unclenched his hands. "Julia Harcourt is a *woman*, and to answer your question, no. I've never known her to be lonely."

Julia might be meant for something bigger and better than small-town Georgia, but during the time she'd lived there, Rhys and his brothers had always made sure she'd never felt alone.

"Not a week after she moved back to Laurel Creek, she reported someone had broken into her home," Sheriff Pearce said. "No signs of forced entry. The locks were intact and nothing was taken except some sheet music."

Rhys kept the newfound information about the Composer's use of the music to himself. "You didn't even follow up on it?"

"There was nothing to follow up on." He paused, then said, "Just like before."

"Before?"

"You know. When she got those letters." Rhys waited for him to elaborate. The sheriff chuckled. "She didn't tell you?"

"Tell me what? What letters are you talking about?"

"About fifteen years ago, Ms. Harcourt reported she'd been receiving disturbing fan letters. Claimed he'd been stalking her. Our investigation ended when evidence suggested she'd sent the letters to herself."

Fifteen years ago? Rhys and she had been dating then. Why had she kept that from him?

Rhys tilted his head. "Why would she have done that?"

The sheriff was just trying to put doubts in Rhys's head about Julia and cause tension between them. Rhys didn't know her reasons for not sharing the letters with him, but he knew one thing for sure. If Julia had told the police she had a stalker, then she had a stalker.

"Julia Harcourt is a performer," Pearce said. "Those kinds of people are always seeking attention. It wasn't right that her parents left her to fend for herself. A child needs rules and discipline. Otherwise, she'll constantly test social boundaries and push societal constraints."

While the sheriff wasn't wrong about Julia's parents, he'd come to the wrong conclusion about Julia. For her, performing had always been about the music, not the attention.

"Sounds to me as if you'd already made up your mind about Ms. Harcourt prior to the recent burglary," Rhys said. "Isn't it possible you were wrong about Julia back then and you're wrong about her now?"

"Isn't it possible you didn't know your girlfriend as well as you thought you did?" Sheriff Pearce didn't wait for a response. "It's a shame about that fourth victim. Must be frustrating to have all those shiny toys and fancy labs at your fingertips and still not be able to solve the case. All investigations start with the people, not evidence. Your dad was always the same way. Looking for evidence. Go with your gut. That's what I do."

Sheriff Pearce's gut was as misguided as the rest of him. If he had taken the threat against Julia seriously from the beginning, he might have stopped a psychopath from killing four innocent women.

Rhys's gut told him Julia's stalker and the recent events were connected.

The glove was practically burning a hole in Rhys's pocket. He was about to point out to the sheriff just how wrong he'd been about Julia when she and Joshua stepped out onto the porch.

"Sheriff, can I offer you a beverage?" she asked, her voice dripping with insincere sweetness.

"No, thank you, Ms. Harcourt." Pearce squared off with Rhys, smug satisfaction etched on his face. "I believe we're done here."

Rhys watched the sheriff leave, not moving an

inch until the car disappeared from view. He'd never liked the man, but after their conversation, he also didn't trust him.

A cup of what was likely sweet tea in his hand, Joshua stepped off the porch and headed toward Rhys. The older brother by two years, Joshua shared the same facial bone structure as Sam and Rhys, but Joshua's nose had a bump along the slope from where Sam had broken it with a basketball. While Rhys and his twin had gotten their mother's straight russet hair and hazel eyes, Joshua had inherited their father's curly black hair and brown eyes. He also claimed to be an inch taller, although Rhys didn't see it.

"I don't know how you can stand to work for him," Rhys said.

"He's a good cop. Yeah, sometimes he can come off a little…insensitive, but he gets the job done."

Rhys wasn't in the mood to shatter his older brother's illusions about the sheriff. Someday soon, Joshua would likely figure it out on his own. "Got something for you." Rhys pulled the glove out of his pocket and handed it to Joshua. "Julia took this off her attacker and he might have left some DNA under her fingernails. Think you could send them both to the local lab for me?"

The guy's carelessness didn't line up with everything Rhys knew about the Composer. With his previous victims, the killer had incapacitated them with an injection of anesthetic prior to abduction. Although Rhys had interrupted him tonight, he'd had time to administer the drug. Instead, he'd given Julia the ability to struggle against him. Why?

Joshua nodded. "No problem. I'll do whatever I can to help."

After he left, Rhys climbed the steps to a waiting Julia. There were things they needed to discuss.

Rhys had questions.

And Julia had the answers.

As Rhys approached, Julia nervously fiddled with the top button of her blouse. He maintained his forward motion until her back was flat against the door. Eyes wide, she swallowed hard. "I guess I'll—"

"Care to explain why you never told me about the letters?"

Julia stilled, the shame in her gaze exposing her guilt.

Before tonight, Rhys had thought he'd known everything there was to know about the teenage Julia Harcourt.

Now he realized he wasn't the only one who'd lied all those years ago.

Chapter Four

"Sheriff Pearce had no right to tell you about the letters." Julia closed the refrigerator door with her hip and poured Rhys an ice-cold glass of sweet tea. Although she'd finally gotten herself to stop trembling, on the inside, she was still a mess, her stomach churning with acid and her mouth as dry as the chicken she'd overcooked the night before. If Rhys hadn't shown up when he had, Julia's night would have ended much differently. *Would she even be alive right now?*

The sheriff's appearance tonight hadn't surprised her. Years ago, he'd made his feelings known. He'd considered her a troublemaker. *Her*, the straight-A student who never broke a rule, the people pleaser. She'd moved back to Georgia with the goal of living a quiet, unassuming existence, and since then, she'd had her house burglarized and was almost kidnapped. The irony of it wasn't lost on her.

"I agree. I shouldn't have learned about the letters from the sheriff. *You* should have told me." Rhys leaned against the kitchen counter, his elbow propped on its fading white Formica top. Having rolled up the sleeves and unbuttoned the top two buttons of his shirt, he looked entirely too comfortable in her house.

In a way, it was as if she and Rhys had stepped back in time. Other than a fresh coat of almond-colored paint on the walls and a couple of new appliances in the kitchen, the interior hadn't changed much since they were children.

There were two entrances to the main room of the house, a door off the front porch and one off the back deck. Tucked into the far left, her kitchen was separated from the living area by a short counter. The natural oak cabinets and the hardwood floors throughout the house memorialized the years with their nicks and scratches. Set underneath her couch and coffee table, a blue-and-white area rug framed the boundaries of her living room. Across from it, she'd placed a four-top square table, used primarily for composing, and her music stand. Playing her violin, she'd stare out the windows at the national forest, watch the deer eat fallen fruit from the trees in her yard and recall all the moments she'd spent with Rhys in those woods. The view had brought her peace.

Now, she couldn't help feeling as if *she* were the one being watched.

Shivers snaked down her nape, then across her shoulder blades, and goose bumps popped up on her arms.

Maybe she should switch from iced to hot tea.

From the opposite side of the counter, she handed Rhys his drink. "Why should I have told you about the letters? They had nothing to do with you," she said, lying through her teeth. This was a conversation she'd tried to avoid for years. On one hand, she was grateful to have Rhys there. She always felt safe whenever she was with him. But on the other hand, being with him dredged up all kinds of emotions from her past, ones she'd hoped would remain buried.

Rhys's eyes brewed with hurt. "How could you say that? I was your boyfriend. We were in—" He stopped and blew out an audible breath. "We were best friends. I thought I knew everything about you."

What had he been about to say?

It didn't matter.

She lowered her gaze to the floor. "Well, you didn't."

"Only because you kept it from me," he said, the hurt from his eyes transferring to his voice so that she couldn't escape it. "Why? Did you think I wouldn't believe you?"

There were so many times she'd almost confided in him, whenever the fear she concealed inside her threatened to overwhelm. But he hadn't needed a friend who came with emotional baggage. He'd had enough of his own.

She looked him in the eyes. "No, of course not." Rhys was nothing like the sheriff. Not then and not now. "You would've believed me, and you would have spent all of your waking moments either worrying about or protecting me."

He frowned. "Yeah, I would have. What's wrong with that?"

"I didn't want to be your obligation," she said. "Between school, football and taking care of your dad, you had enough on your plate. You were still coming to terms with your mom's death, and I worried it would trigger you. When I was with you, I was just a normal teenager. I wanted a few hours when I could pretend I was just like everyone else we went to school with."

"No matter how hard you tried, you were never like everyone else." He grabbed her hand, leading her around the counter and to the couch. "Tell me about the letters, Julia."

Disentangling their fingers, she sat beside him, close enough to feel his body heat but far enough so as not to touch. She smoothed her palms down the fabric of her skirt, trying to decide where to begin. Once she allowed herself to remember, all the fear and anxiety from those years rushed to the surface, souring her stomach. "I got my first letter the day of my fourteenth birthday and about one a month after that. There was nothing threatening about them. They were the opposite, in fact. The letters praised me for my talent. He... I say 'he,' but there's nothing in the letters that substantiates the writer's gender—it's just a feeling I have when I read them. He said I would be revered as one of the greatest violinists of the twenty-first century."

Glancing at Rhys's hands as she gathered the

strength to continue, she noted his ragged fingernails. It comforted her to realize the boy she used
to know, the one who couldn't stop his nail biting
habit no matter how hard he tried, was still inside
that body of a man. "At first, I was flattered, but then
the tone changed."

"Changed how?" he prodded gently.

"The flattery bordered on obsessive. He put me
on a pedestal so high there wasn't a chance I could
meet the expectations. That's when Daniel took me
to the sheriff to report it." Daniel Fenske had been
more than her violin teacher; he'd been a father figure to her. Initially, she'd kept him in the dark, but
after he'd accidentally opened one of the envelopes
and read its contents, she'd had no choice. "Sheriff
Pearce called them fan letters. He didn't think there
was anything to investigate, but Daniel forced the
issue. Two weeks later, the sheriff knocked on my
door at home and accused me of sending the letters
to myself. That was the end of that."

Rhys's nostrils flared and his lips curled into a
snarl. "Did he give you any reason for his conclusions?"

She rolled her eyes. Immature, she knew, but the
sheriff brought it out in her. "Only that most of the
letters weren't mailed and others were mailed locally.
They were either left in my box at home or mixed in
with the mail at the symphony. He didn't even bother
comparing my handwriting to the letters."

At best, Sheriff Pearce was a fool. At worst, a misogynist. She hadn't understood that as a teenager, but as an adult, she recognized his treatment toward her had revictimized her.

Chilly from both the air conditioner and the memories, she rubbed her palms on her skirt. "He made it clear that there was nothing illegal about sending someone a fan letter, but it was illegal to file a false report. After that, I kept the letters to myself. Even when…"

Rhys nabbed the blanket hanging on the edge of the couch and spread it over her lap. "When what?"

His considerate response to her physical discomfort didn't surprise her. It was one of the things that had made her fall in love with him when they were younger.

"I fell from the pedestal." She remembered the day they'd changed. She had been walking on a cloud all week, happier than she'd ever been, and then she'd read the letter. "He was so angry at me. He said I deserved to suffer."

All she'd wanted to do was run to Rhys and have him take care of everything. But what if he decided they should break up? Even then, she'd known he'd do whatever it took to keep her safe. If he'd believed dating him put her at risk, he'd end their relationship for her sake.

Rhys shifted on the couch, angling his body toward her. "What set him off? How did you fall from the pedestal?"

How did she tell him without him blaming himself? Years had passed, but that didn't mean that

Rhys would take the news any better. The difference was they were no longer together. Now he wouldn't protect her because of love.

Protecting her had become his duty.

He was quiet as he waited for her response. She saw the moment comprehension dawned. "Me." A muscle in his jaw contracted. "It happened when you and I became more than just friends."

She nodded. "Yes."

She and Rhys had gone to their favorite spot on the trail to celebrate finishing their freshman year. Splashing and roughhousing in the pond had led to their first kiss underneath the waterfall. Her heart had been pounding so hard, she'd thought she'd pass out. As evidenced by tonight, her body's reaction to having Rhys near hadn't changed.

How ironic that her first time seeing Rhys in twelve years happened to be mere feet from where they'd shared their first and last kiss. Was it any surprise that her body had gotten confused when Rhys had lain on top of it?

"You shouldn't have kept the letters a secret," Rhys said, his voice tight. "You should have told me. I would've helped."

She didn't understand why he cared so much. It was in the past. "It's irrelevant now. They stopped when I moved."

He leaned forward and took her hand. "I don't think that's true, Julia."

Her stomach churned as the implication of his

words sunk in. "You think the person who wrote the letters is the same person who attacked me tonight?"

It wasn't as if she hadn't considered the possibility her return might catch the notice of her stalker, but she figured it was unlikely. More than twelve years had passed without incident. It wasn't as if her stalker couldn't have found her address in Europe. She'd received plenty of fan mail throughout the years. Even a couple of threatening messages. But none in the handwriting she'd grown all too familiar with in Georgia. Why didn't he hurt her all those years ago? Why start now?

Rhys's expression turned grim. "Not only do I think the person who wrote the letters attacked you tonight, I think he broke into your house, stole your composition and is killing women who remind him of you. I think he'll keep killing until he can get what he really wants..." A muscle twitched in his cheek as he swallowed. "You."

Her stomach's churning turned into full-blown nausea. She ripped her hand away from Rhys to cover her mouth and popped up from the couch. She crossed the room to the window. Rationally, she knew she wasn't responsible for the deaths of the other women, but that wasn't enough to keep the guilt from suffusing her entire being. If only she had done something differently, the women might still be alive. Some psycho had targeted those women because of *her*.

Staring out into the darkness, she curled her fingers into the palms of her hands. No, she wouldn't let herself take the blame for a killer's actions. It wasn't her fault. All she had done was return to Laurel Creek. "I know you probably think I should leave," she said, still looking out the window, "but I refuse to allow the Composer to drive me from my home."

She didn't hear Rhys walk up behind her, but she felt his heat at her back before he spoke. "As long as the Composer is out there, you're not safe. But I understand how you feel. Which is why I'm going to stay here with you."

His pronouncement struck her like a punch to the gut, creating an ache between her ribs. "No. No way. Absolutely not."

Having him there in her space, night after night, would make it much more difficult to remember the makeshift boundary she'd created to protect herself between Rhys the FBI agent and Rhys the ordinary man. Even now, she wanted nothing more than for him to wrap his arms around her and kiss away her fears. In some ways, Rhys was even more dangerous to her than the Composer.

Rhys reached around her to lower the shade, his head bent just right that he murmured in her ear. "Have you always been this obstinate, or is this a new development?"

Before he got the chance to feel the shivers the rumble in his voice sent throughout her body, Julia whirled around and pushed him back with both hands to his chest. "What you and others call *obstinate* is what I like to think of as *independent*."

His brows dipped. "You've always been independent. You practically raised yourself."

Shaking her head, she laughed bitterly. "Me, independent? Do you know what it's like to have no say over your own life? To have people micromanaging every little aspect of your day so that the only decision you have to make is whether to drink flat or sparkling water with dinner? Until recently, that was what it was like for me. It's always been like that for me."

"You never said anything."

Even when she'd lived in Laurel Creek as a teenager, she'd had few choices in how she lived her life. Maybe that's what had attracted her to the Keller boys. They'd taken a lonely girl and had shown her what it would be like to have autonomy in her life.

She dropped her head to her chest. "How could I complain when your family had gone through so much?"

Despite their family tragedy, the three of them had lived every moment to the fullest. They'd been popular in school, never missed a party and still managed to get good grades. She'd envied that, while at the same time, she'd understood they each carried a darkness within them as a result of losing their mother, Alicia, to murder, and their father, Griffin, to grief.

"Hey." He moved closer and lifted her chin. "It

was never a contest of who had it rougher. At least I had my brothers."

Warmth permeated throughout her chest. "Hanging with you, Sam and Joshua was the only time I felt like I could just be. I didn't only come back to Laurel Creek for a job. I came to find myself again. And if that means being obstinate, so be it."

The right side of his mouth lifted in a lopsided grin, reminding Julia of a teenage Rhys. "You don't need my approval, but you have it. Still, there's a difference between obstinate and inflexible. Which is why I'm giving you a choice. The Bureau put me up at a hotel about a half hour from here, so that I don't have to make the drive between Laurel Creek and my apartment in Atlanta every day. I can either get you a room at my hotel, or I'm staying here." His thumb caressed the underside of her chin. "What's it gonna be, Julia?"

Pretending his touch wasn't causing her pulse to race, she considered her options. It would be irrational to insist she stay alone in her house. A hotel was the safer option for more reasons than one. But she'd meant what she said. She wasn't going to let the Composer scare her from her home.

She sighed. "Fine. You can stay here."

A glint in Rhys's eyes told her he'd known what she'd choose all along. He dropped his hand to his side. "Thank you for compromising."

What he considered a compromise, she'd call the

lesser evil to an ultimatum. She just hoped she didn't live to regret it.

Although Rhys no longer touched her, he remained where he stood—which was way too close for comfort. Needing space, she took a step back and pivoted her body in the direction of the kitchen. "You must be hungry. Can I make you something to eat?"

"No. I'm good. I should probably get some sleep. It's been a long day."

"Right." She couldn't imagine the toll investigating a serial killer took on him. "Do you need to call FBI headquarters to let them know you're staying here? What about a change of clothes? Do you need to get anything from your car?"

"I'll get my suitcase in the morning." Rhys smiled. "If I didn't know better, I would think you were stalling."

About to protest, she stopped herself, realizing he was right. "Let me make up the bed for you."

"You don't have to go to any trouble. I can just crash on the couch."

Rhys's frame would barely fit her couch. He deserved better. As did the victims of the Composer. It wouldn't do anyone any good if the lead agent was tired and sore after a bad night's sleep. Besides, she had an extra bedroom for him. "It's no trouble."

She led him into the room that used to be hers and flicked on the light. Even as a kid, she hadn't plastered her wall with posters of rock stars or the usual teenage heartthrobs. Instead, she'd hung framed prints of her favorite violin paintings.

They were still there.

So was her antique bedroom set, the white wood dresser, nightstand and twin bed all etched with scrolls and hearts. It was as if her past had been frozen in time.

Rhys put his hands on his hips and rocked back on his heels. "Wow. This brings back memories." Grinning, he jutted his chin toward the window. "Only this time, I finally get to sleep in your bed."

She laughed, her cheeks heating. She and Rhys definitely had taken advantage of her guardian's early bedtime. How many times had he snuck in through that window? Enough that she'd double-checked its security after the break-in. But he'd never spent the night. "Mine's in the master bedroom."

It was odd to take the room that had belonged to her parents even though they'd only stayed in it a couple of times, too busy touring the world to settle down for more than a few days at a time. Still, she'd bought a new mattress for the bed and swapped out the artwork for the paintings she'd brought back from Paris.

The thought of Rhys sleeping in her old bed was oddly erotic.

But thoughts like that were dangerous. She couldn't go down that road again. She wouldn't survive a second round of loving and losing Rhys, especially since her heart had never quite healed from the first time. Before they'd become more, Rhys had been her friend.

Her best friend. As much as she found herself still attracted to him, it was his friendship she missed the most. She would just think of him as a friend.

And there was nothing erotic about a friend sleeping in her old bed.

Repeating the word *friend* over and over in her mind, she opened the closet and grabbed a set of cotton sheets from the shelf. She carried them over to the queen-size bed and started the process of putting on the fitted sheet. As it always seemed to do, one side of the sheet popped off while working on the opposite side. Hair falling into her eyes, she leaned over the mattress to reattach it.

"Here, let me help," Rhys offered.

His voice sounded a bit raspier than normal, and Julia's cheeks heated as she realized why.

Flustered, she released the sheet to yank down the bottom edge of her skirt and reared up, colliding into Rhys. She wobbled, off-balance, surprised by his nearness. His hands bracketed her hips, steadying her. Her body shivered even though her insides were warming.

He slowly turned her.

The heat banked in his eyes had her wanting to forget the mantra she'd repeated to herself only minutes before. As his lips descended, she couldn't catch her breath. Friends kissed, right? What would be the harm? His mouth hovered mere centimeters from hers when the answer to that question slammed her back into reality.

A broken heart.

Turning her head to the side, she pushed gently against his shoulders. "I'm sorry. I can't do this."

A beat passed before he blew out a breath and took a giant step back. "You're right. You're a witness in my case. It wouldn't be professional."

She agreed. So why was she disappointed he didn't argue with her?

Shaking her head as if the action would wipe the emotion away, she set herself to finish making the bed. Rhys made good on his offer and helped, staying on the opposite side of the mattress from her and ensuring they wouldn't bump into each other again.

It was for the best.

Recalling Rhys had lowered the shade in the other room, she glanced at the window. Her home used to be her sanctuary, but now, with all of its windows, she felt as if were a caged tiger on display at the zoo. "Do you think he's watching?"

He closed the drapes. "I wish I could say he isn't, but I don't know. Keep all the windows covered. I'm going to keep you safe, Julia. I promise."

She knew he would.

He always had. If there was one thing she didn't doubt, it was that Rhys would do anything to protect her.

Even break her heart.

Chapter Five

After a restless night's sleep and another one of his recurring nightmares about Julia drowning in a lake, Rhys was surprisingly wide-awake. It could have been due to a rush of adrenaline in response to the new leads in his investigation. Or—the more likely scenario—it could have been due to the beautiful woman at his side.

Outside the symphony's entrance, Julia attempted once again to convince Rhys his presence wasn't necessary. "I don't need a chaperone, Rhys," she repeated for the third time that morning. "No one is going to hurt me in the presence of eighty people. I'll be safe here."

He wasn't caving, especially not after learning the name of yesterday's victim and the manner of how she'd been taken. Cindy Phillips, age twenty-eight, had been at a county fair with a group of friends when she disappeared, proving Julia's crowd of eighty wouldn't protect her. "You're right. You will be safe here. Because I'm staying to make sure of it."

Nothing in Laurel Creek had changed much since the last time Rhys had accompanied Julia to the symphony. Located a block off Main Street, the beautiful building was the oldest one in Laurel Creek, first used as a church before it had been converted into a symphony hall fifty years ago in an attempt to turn the financially weakened town into a vacation spot. The rest of the downtown had developed around it, Main Street now peppered by charming shops owned by locals who sold anything from sweets to crafts to Christmas decor.

In addition to the boutique hotels in the area, outside investors bought homes and fixed them up as bed-and-breakfasts. With access to the nearby state and federal parks, as well as mountains and rivers, Laurel Creek became one of the top year-round tourist spots in Georgia. And the Laurel Creek Symphony was considered the town's crown jewel. Although it wasn't located in a major city, the symphony was rated in the country's top ten. It was a draw that brought in wealthy tourists seeking a ticket to an off-the-beaten-path cultural experience.

Julia pursed her lips, drawing attention to her mouth and reminding Rhys of what he'd almost done to it. "You must have more important things to do than play bodyguard all day."

If she hadn't stopped him, he would've kissed her last night. Having his hands on her, breathing in the scent of her, he'd forgotten himself in that moment. It was as if the last twelve years had never happened and it was just the two of them against the world. Before he'd come to his senses and freed her from the inevitable darkness that followed him. Two months back in Laurel Creek and Julia had already become entangled in it.

Being in her presence was like being near a fire. Its flames provided warmth and light, but get too close, and there was a risk of getting burned. And both of them would have gone up in flames until nothing was left but ashes.

She should have never come back.

If anything, her return only proved he'd been right to break up with her in the first place.

He forced his gaze away from her mouth and held open the symphony's lobby door for her. "I have other reasons for being here."

"You can't possibly think someone I work with is responsible for my attack last night or the deaths of those women," she said to him over her shoulder as she strolled inside. "They're musicians like me. Hardly the type to commit murder."

"One thing I learned in my years working for the FBI is everyone is the type," he muttered. "People aren't always what they seem."

"Not in my experience."

She was lucky. He hadn't been as fortunate. Other than his brothers and Julia, he didn't trust a single soul. Monsters could hide inside of anyone.

The sound of Julia's high heels echoed throughout the lobby with every step on the black-and-white marble floor. Rhys had always marveled at the lavish interior of the symphony hall. Each time he visited, he noticed something new. With its high ceilings adorned by frescoes reminiscent of the Sistine Chapel, the lobby had remained virtually the same as when it was used as a church. At the back of the lobby, the crimson-carpeted grand staircase led to the orchestra-level seating, and behind the staircase was the entrance to the main floor. Every one of the two thousand lush velvet-cushioned seats had the perfect view of the stage, as well as the gold pillars lining the walls and the crystal chandelier hanging from the middle of the round ceiling.

The symphony's members typically used the staff-only entrance located at the back of the building, but since Rhys had accompanied Julia today, she'd insisted they use the lobby entrance. Julia had always been a stickler for the rules. It amused him to see that hadn't changed.

Passing the grand staircase, Rhys spotted two men having what appeared to be a heated discussion just outside the theater doors. Although he hadn't seen him in more than a decade, he immediately recognized the older man. A few more lines graced his oblong face, and his hair was more salt than pepper now, but he'd kept the same short side-part style, which accentuated his thin pointed nose and bushy eyebrows. The younger guy with the square jaw looked familiar, but Rhys couldn't place him. He wore wire-rimmed glasses with round lenses and used too much gel in his slicked-back strawberry blond hair. Rhys guessed he was around his and Julia's age.

As Rhys and Julia approached, the younger one stormed off with a scowl on his face. Fenske, on the other hand, smiled welcomingly.

"Rhys, you remember Maestro Fenske," Julia said. "He was my music tutor and the assistant conductor of the orchestra back then. Now, the Laurel Creek Symphony is privileged to call him conductor and music director."

The six-foot-tall Rhys shook his hand, noting that the man was a couple inches taller than himself. "Of course. Good to see you again, Maestro."

"Please, call me Daniel. You're an adult now," he said teasingly. "What brings you by today? Come to see Julia rehearse?"

"I'm here on a professional matter."

"Rhys is a special agent with the FBI. He's investigating the murders of those women found on the trails." Julia glanced at Rhys before turning her attention to Daniel. "Do you remember those letters I used to get?"

Daniel's bushy eyebrows furrowed as he frowned. "Hard to forget a thing like that. For a short time, they continued to come even after you left. Very disturbing."

"Rhys thinks there might be a connection between the letters and the murders."

"What kind of connection? Julia, are you in danger?"

"No—"

"Yes," Rhys said. It was important for those who cared about Julia to know the truth. "It's possible Julia might be a target, especially in light of last night's occurrence."

Julia pivoted her body toward him, her eyes flashing with annoyance.

"Last night?" Daniel asked, his gaze ping-ponging between Julia and Rhys.

"Someone attacked Julia in her driveway. Unfortunately, he got away." Although her attacker had been shorter than Rhys, and therefore, shorter than Daniel, he had to do his due diligence. "I'm sorry to have to ask, but where were you last night at ten p.m.?"

"Here, doing paperwork."

"Alone?"

"Rhys!" Julia elbowed Rhys in the ribs. "I'm sorry, Daniel."

Rhys put a hand on Julia's shoulder and spoke softly. "I know you're protective of him and everyone else at the symphony, but you have to let me do my job."

"You're right." She raised her chin defiantly. "I have a job to do as well. If you'll excuse me, I'm going to go warm up." On that note, Julia strode through the main floor doors of the theater, leaving Rhys and Daniel alone.

"It's good to have her back, isn't it?" Daniel beamed with pride. "Come with me. We can speak in my office."

Rhys accompanied Daniel down a long hallway

that ran along the length of the theater to the back of the building, located behind the stage. Unlike the lobby and the symphony hall, the office area had seen better days, its white walls yellowing with age and its carpet worn and stained.

He'd only been back there one other time, when Julia had gotten the flu and had been too ill to walk to the car. Because Julia's guardian had been out of town visiting family, Daniel had allowed Rhys to carry her to his car and take her home with him, where Rhys had nursed her to health over the period of a few days. Her parents had been worried, but not enough to come home. In fact, on their phone call with Rhys, they'd expressed how grateful they were to Rhys.

That's when it had really hit him how alone Julia had been.

Daniel flipped on the lights to his office. It wasn't much larger than the old one he'd been in as assistant conductor. Rhys would have thought his current position would require more space, but he supposed Daniel spent the majority of his time conducting rather than sitting behind his messy desk. There was a metal file cabinet tucked in the left corner, and beside it, a black leather couch, the same one Julia had been sleeping on when Rhys had found her feverish and coughing from the flu. There was also a kitchenette tucked in the right corner.

"To answer your earlier question," Daniel said, "I was not alone here last night. My assistant, Penelope, was here as well. If you'd like to speak with her, she should be in later this afternoon."

Rhys leaned his back against the wall. "I'll make sure to do that. No offense meant."

Daniel waved a hand. "No offense taken. You're only doing your job. Unlike that sheriff of ours."

"Not a fan of his?"

"He never took Julia's stalker seriously. I expressed my concerns with him more than once, but it had been clear he'd made up his mind and nothing would change it. A couple of letters arrived here with a local postmark after she left town. I brought them to the sheriff's office to prove Julia hadn't been sending them to herself. He took the letters from me, but rather than admit he'd been wrong, he told me it no longer mattered because they'd closed her file since she was no longer a resident. I got one more letter after that. Instead of handing it over to the sheriff, I kept it in my desk. No matter how many years have passed, I've never been able to forget the cruelty laced in the words."

It was bad enough that Pearce had disregarded a teenage Julia's stalker claims, but to also ignore the word of a highly regarded adult member of the community bordered on recklessness. Rhys would like to think if his father had still been sheriff, he would have taken her seriously.

"Other than you, who knew Julia was coming back to Laurel Creek?" Rhys asked.

"I didn't keep it a secret. As soon as she called, I made the announcement to the symphony members."

"When was that?"

"About two months ago." Daniel crossed to his desk. "Let me get you that letter." He opened a drawer and searched through a stack full of papers. Rhys got the sense he wasn't very organized. "Here it is." Hand outstretched, he passed it to Rhys. "I need to get to rehearsal. Feel free to stay and use my office." Daniel walked toward the exit but turned around just inside the doorway. "Rhys… I'm glad you and Julia have reconnected. Take care of her."

"I won't let anyone harm her," Rhys vowed.

Daniel nodded, his expression somber. "I hope you're including yourself when you say that. Because you, more than anyone, have the power to hurt her."

That was the last thing Rhys wanted to do. That's why he'd broken up with her all those years ago. Keeping himself from holding her, touching her, kissing her would prove difficult, but he'd done it before and he would do it again. When he finally caught the Composer and ensured Julia was safe, he'd leave again. With her job and Daniel there to support her, she'd be okay. She'd move on. And Rhys would go on loving her from a distance, just as he had since he'd lied to her in order to convince her to go to Europe.

Rhys dropped into the chair behind Daniel's desk and read the letter. The writing was in cursive and printed in black ink. There was nothing that stood out about the paper or the penmanship, but he wasn't an expert. There was a whole division of experts in the FBI who would have a field day with the letter.

The contents of it were far darker than Julia had let on. In it, the author described all the ways he wanted to kill her, down to the most intricate detail. Rhys had seen a lot of death in his lifetime, but the letter was particularly disturbing—especially since it was written for Julia. Getting inside the mind of a serial killer was no easy task, but a firsthand account of the inner workings of a psychopath's mind was catnip to the BAU. Hopefully, from this letter, they'd be able to fine-tune the Composer's profile and narrow down the suspects for him.

Rhys's gut roiled from his guilt. Someone, somewhere—likely nearby—was fantasizing about torturing and killing Julia. With each victim, the responsibility weighed heavier on Rhys's shoulders. But none of it compared to how he felt knowing Julia could be next.

Rhys clenched his fist as he pushed up from the desk and headed toward the theater.

His father never said it outright, but Rhys knew he believed he'd failed their mother, first in allowing her to be murdered and then in neglecting to find her killer. Rhys had always resented him for it. While his father had lost himself in grief, Rhys and his brothers had been left to fend for themselves.

With Julia's life at risk, Rhys now understood what drove his father to become obsessed over his wife's murder. If the worst happened to Julia—Rhys could barely stand to think it—he'd be exactly like his father.

He would not fail her.

Curving around the hallway onto the back part of the stage, Rhys spotted the same guy from earlier. A flicker of recognition flared. Lewis Vogel. He'd been another one of Daniel's violin students when they were teens. As hard as Julia had tried to make friends with him, he'd only seen her as a rival. Julia had taken it personally until Rhys convinced her of the truth about Lewis. He was just a jealous jerk.

Apparently, nothing had changed. Lewis was complaining to a few of the other musicians.

And he wasn't being quiet about it.

"Ten years I've played here professionally," Lewis said, "paying my dues, working my way up to first chair, and Julia just waltzes back into town, and the first chair is hers."

Years ago, Julia had explained to Rhys about the coveted first chair. Also called the concertmaster, the person was considered the best of the section. They sat to the left of the conductor and were tasked with the duty to tune the symphony before a concert.

"I don't know why I'm surprised. Fenske and her have been lovers since she was a teen. Guess it pays to sleep with the conductor."

Red-hot rage consumed Rhys. "You're lying."

He didn't stop to think. He just charged. Pinning the guy to the wall with one hand, Rhys wrapped his other around his throat in a less than subtle threat. In the back of his mind, he knew this was a bad idea, but he couldn't stop himself.

Lewis's eyes popped wide. Even though Rhys wasn't squeezing his throat, Lewis acted as if he couldn't breathe, hyperventilating in fear. Lewis lifted both hands up in surrender. "I didn't..."

A bandage snagged Rhys's attention. Releasing his grip on Lewis, he took a step back. "What happened to your hand?"

Lewis shrugged, glancing at the white gauze wrapped around his palm. "I cut it making dinner last night."

"Anyone who can verify that claim?"

"No. I live alone, and it wasn't bad enough to go to the hospital to get stitches." Lewis scowled. "What's your problem?"

"My problem? My problem is you. Julia was attacked in her driveway last night, and you just became my number one suspect."

"Suspect in what?"

Rhys pulled out his ID and flashed it in front of Lewis's face. "FBI special agent. I'm investigating a series of homicides you might have heard about. The Composer ring a bell?"

Lewis had motive. Julia had been his competition when they'd been teens. He'd benefited by her move to Europe only to be relegated to second chair upon Julia's return to the symphony.

Lewis had opportunity. He'd been a fellow student

of Daniel's when Julia had received the letters and had learned about her return to the symphony two months ago, before the murders began.

There was evidence implicating him. Granted, it was circumstantial at the moment, but Lewis didn't have an alibi for the time when Julia had been attacked, and his right hand was injured, the same side Julia had scratched on her attacker last night. Not to mention, being several inches shorter than Rhys, Lewis matched the attacker's height.

"I didn't kill anyone," Lewis said, fear leaking into his voice. "Honest. I would never—"

Rhys got up in Lewis's face. "I remember you from high school. You were always jealous of Julia, but you wanted her just the same, didn't you? And she shot you down. Is that why you started writing her those letters?"

Lewis's neck craned left and right as he searched around for help. All of his cohorts had disappeared as soon as Rhys had flashed his credentials. "What letters? I don't know anything about any letters. You've got it wrong, Keller."

If Lewis Vogel was the Composer, it wouldn't take much to break him. Rhys didn't have to be a psychologist to know Lewis was the kind of person who felt stronger by demeaning others, but in actuality, he was weak.

Rhys's cell rang from his pocket. He checked the caller, saw it was Joshua. "Good timing. I'm bringing in a suspect for questioning."

"Rhys, there's been another murder."

Looked like Lewis would have to wait. "I'm on my way."

AFTER A DEPUTY SHERIFF arrived to guard Julia in his absence, Rhys walked the few blocks from the symphony hall to the high school and crossed the football field toward the edge of the woods. The previous Composer victims had been found along the national trails, which was why Rhys was surprised to hear Joshua's news.

It was another scorcher of a day, with temperatures well into the high eighties, and it wasn't yet 10:00 a.m. The sun beat down on the back of his neck, sweat trickling down underneath the collar of his shirt. He spotted Joshua speaking to a female deputy, who was nodding at whatever he was saying.

It was obvious to Rhys that although Pearce was technically the person in charge of the sheriff's office, Joshua was truly in command. It hadn't escaped Rhys's attention that although Pearce denied the correlation between Julia and the Composer, Joshua had managed to arrange for the deputies to guard Julia. Rhys couldn't imagine he did so with Pearce's blessing. Unlike Rhys's father had been when sheriff, Pearce seemed like more of a politician than a cop. He was more concerned with keeping his job than doing it.

As Rhys ducked under the crime tape, a handful of reporters shouted questions at him. He ignored them and headed toward his brother. "What have we got?"

Joshua handed him a set of booties and gloves to keep from contaminating the crime scene, then turned and walked into the woods. "We haven't confirmed the victim's identity, but based on the description of what she was wearing the night she disappeared, and the advanced decay of the body, the victim is most likely Diana Crain, age twenty, a local who went missing two months ago. She hadn't been seen since she disappeared walking back home from her job at the antique shop on Main around 9:00 p.m."

Rhys quickly donned the gear and followed right behind him. There wasn't a trail or even an official path in there. The woods were within the school's property boundaries, which gave the Laurel Creek School District primary responsibility for maintaining them. Trespassers and students were explicitly forbidden from entering the woods, but school rules and posted signs weren't enough to prevent students from doing it anyway. It was a not-so-secret place to hang with friends during the school year. As a result, there were clearings where tree branches had been broken off and bushes had been trampled on, creating makeshift paths throughout the woods. The forest was accessible from three different streets and the school's football field. Because it was located in the center of town, dozens of people passed by the woods every day.

The antique shop was located at the far west end

of Main. "That's only a half mile from here. Anyone see her on her way home?"

"No," Joshua said, pushing a branch out of their way. "It's possible Diana was picked up by someone. She didn't have her own car or a driver's license. But she called her parents right before she left to let them know she was on her way home."

"What makes you think this homicide is related to the Composer?"

"You'll see."

The stench of death hit him as they neared the crime scene. It had taken him years to become immune to the smell, but the deputies around him weren't as experienced with decaying bodies—that included his brother. Joshua's face paled. Bent over with a fist to his mouth, Joshua coughed, probably fighting against his gag reflex. Knowing this couldn't be easy on him, Rhys waited patiently for his brother.

Joshua exhaled shakily, then straightened. "I'm good. Let's go."

Less than a minute later, they came to a small clearing, where a crowd of law enforcement officers diligently processed the scene. Rhys ignored them all, too focused on the young woman responsible for their presence.

Facedown, the body was half buried underneath a pile of dirt, branches and leaves. Even without seeing her face, there was no missing that she matched the other victims physically. At the same time, there was nothing else to indicate the work of the Composer. "There's no tattoo."

"No, and the body wasn't staged on a trail. Based on how he buried her, whoever did this, he didn't want her found. Or at least, he didn't care if she was. It's not the same MO as the Composer. Probably not the same guy." Joshua rocked back on his heels. "Only…"

"Only your gut is screaming like mine that it probably *is* the same guy." What were the chances there were two people killing young blonde women in the local area and positioning them facedown in the woods?

Rhys couldn't be sure until the autopsy, but based on the condition of her body, she was likely killed shortly after disappearing. Two months ago, Julia was still in Europe. The Composer hadn't stolen Julia's composition yet. That could be the reason for the lack of a tattoo. And a criminal's MO evolved over time.

"She could be his first victim," Joshua suggested, as if reading his brother's mind. "That would account for the difference in MO. Think her body was dumped here?"

If it had been during the school year, her body would have been found quickly. Students were notorious for using those woods to drink, smoke and engage in other adult activities. Since it was summer and students generally didn't want to hang out near their school, they partied in a different part of town, leaving those woods unused from June to August. Anyone who lived in town would know that.

Rhys looked around, assessing. "I think it was a crime of opportunity. Have the coroner check if she was injected with an anesthetic to make her more compliant like the other victims." The Composer might not have needed it if she'd trusted him. She might have even gone into the woods willingly. It would explain why no one heard her scream for help, and why he hadn't staged her body. If he'd known her, he might have felt guilt. Unlike the others he'd killed, he hadn't wanted Diana to be found. "Two months ago, Daniel Fenske made an announcement to the symphony members that Julia would be joining them. From there, word would have spread. Everyone in Laurel Creek would have heard."

Joshua put his hands on his hips. "So, you're thinking it set him off? He learned Julia was coming back and turned his anger on Diana?"

"It's a theory," Rhys said, being careful. He didn't want to jump the gun. "But as of now, there's not enough to link this homicide to the Composer. That means the sheriff's office retains its jurisdiction."

"I'm glad to hear you say so, Special Agent Keller," Sheriff Pearce said, sauntering up to stand between Rhys and Joshua. There wasn't a drop of sweat on the man. He'd obviously just gotten there. Wouldn't surprise Rhys if he had arrived just in time to do his press conference for all the waiting cameras.

"I called him, Sheriff," Joshua admitted. "I thought he—"

"You thought wrong, Captain." Pearce turned his

back to Joshua, speaking to Rhys directly. "FBI has no business being here at this crime scene. This is a local matter."

Rhys couldn't argue that. He could appeal to the sheriff's reasonable side—if he had one. "This woman physically matches the Composer's victims."

"Lots of women do. Are you going to pay a visit to every crime scene with a blonde girl?"

"If I have to." Rhys would do his job, even if it meant a lifetime of sleepless nights. "How are you certain this woman's homicide isn't related to my case?"

The sheriff's phone buzzed in his hand. "Until the results come back from her autopsy, we don't know this even *is* a homicide." Lifting it to eye level, he read the message and typed a reply. "Or does the FBI prefer to work on theories rather than evidence?"

If Pearce wanted to talk about theories versus evidence, Rhys could recite all the ways the sheriff had ignored evidence in Julia's stalking case based on his theory that Julia had invented it all because she'd been lonely.

"You know as well as I do that Diana Crain didn't die from natural causes." It wasn't as if she buried herself.

Pearce sighed and tucked his phone into his back pocket. "Even so, there's no reason for you to be here at my crime scene. The sheriff's office will be processing the evidence and doing the subsequent investigation into her death. Owen Baker, Diana's boyfriend, has been our primary suspect in her disappearance, and nothing has changed. Now that she's been found, his arrest is likely imminent."

Joshua hadn't mentioned that to him. Rhys glanced at his brother, whose expression didn't change. He wasn't giving anything away while the sheriff was standing there. "I'd like to interview him."

Sheriff Pearce grunted. "No need. If we discover anything relevant to your case, we'll let you know. Otherwise, stay away from things that have nothing to do with you. Don't make the same mistake as Griffin. Learn from your brother instead." Eyeing Joshua, he raised his brow. "With the exception of calling you today, he usually knows his place." Then apparently having said his piece, Pearce strode away to speak with the coroner.

Once he was out of earshot, Rhys confronted his brother. "Is he right? Do you know your place, Joshua?"

Joshua grinned smugly. "Don't worry about Pearce. I've got it covered."

Rhys had never been prouder of him. "Tell me how I can find Owen Baker."

His brother scratched his bearded cheek. "Well now, that's going to be a problem."

"Why?"

Joshua's answer was written all over his face. "Because Owen Baker has gone missing."

Chapter Six

If Julia never rode in a sheriff's vehicle again, it would be too soon. At the end of rehearsal, the sheriff's deputy had informed Julia that she'd be taking her home. Reason and logic apparently weren't enough to convince the deputy to allow Daniel to do it. Everyone watched as Julia was ushered out of the hall and into the deputy's work vehicle. At least Julia had been permitted to ride in the front. Thank goodness for small favors. Still, it had been unnecessary. She didn't blame the deputy. No, she'd just been doing her job.

Julia blamed Rhys.

Rhys, who had left her at the symphony without saying a word. It hadn't been until the sheriff's deputy had introduced herself to Julia during a fifteen-minute break that she'd even known he'd gone.

It hadn't helped that Lewis continually glared at her all through rehearsal. When she'd asked him why, he'd told her, "Ask your boyfriend."

And she would.

As soon as he came home.

After work, she'd made herself a sandwich and soup for dinner, then settled on her couch with a book she'd been eager to find time to read. By page ten, she realized she hadn't comprehended a word of it. Between wondering where Rhys had gone and what he had done or said to make Lewis so angry, she was too distracted to sit still.

Other than running—which was impossible to do right then since it was dark out and there was a killer on the loose—only one activity quieted her mind.

She removed her violin from its case and caressed the smooth, cool spruce wood of the top. When all else failed, she always had music. It had gotten her through the worst of times, including the days following her breakup with Rhys. As long as she had her violin with her, she was never alone.

Choosing a modern piece to play, she stood by the shade-covered window and got lost in the magic of music. The light soprano timbre filled the room. Her fingers ached from the hours of rehearsal, but she didn't mind. The ache made her feel alive.

A thud cut through the sound of her bow sliding across the strings.

Startled, she froze.

"Hello?" she called out.

She didn't move a muscle as she waited for a reply. She didn't even swallow.

The house was silent.

If it were any other time, she wouldn't have thought

twice about a strange noise. She wouldn't have even paused her playing. But it wasn't any other time. She couldn't assume it was the wind or a branch falling off a tree. Assumptions could get her killed.

Her pulse fluttered in her neck and her breathing quickened. She rested her violin and bow on the table and crept as quietly as she could into the kitchen to grab her largest and sharpest knife. The noise sounded as if it had come from one of the bedrooms.

The deputy was sitting in her car right outside, guarding the house.

Julia just had to walk out the front door to get to her.

Knife in hand, she held her breath and ran toward the exit. She flipped the locks and threw open the door.

A dark figure blocked her exit. She didn't have time to process it. Her survival instinct kicked in, and she raised her knife before the Composer had the chance to attack.

The knife sliced through the air.

A large hand clamped her wrist, capturing her arm midair. "Julia! It's me!"

She lifted her gaze to Rhys's face. His eyes were wide with shock, mirroring what she was feeling.

She had almost stabbed him.

Julia blew out a shaky breath, the adrenaline from the scare still coursing through her blood. She took a step back to allow him through the door. "I thought I heard a noise. And, well, never mind. I overreacted."

She chuffed out a nervous laugh. "It must have been you." The thud had probably been Rhys slamming his car door shut.

Rhys closed the door behind him and locked it. When he turned back around, his gaze fixed on her hand. "You can put the knife down now, Julia," he said softly.

She looked down, surprised, not realizing it was still in her grip. "Right. Sorry." Embarrassed, she unraveled her fingers from the tight hold she had on the handle and scurried to return it to the kitchen drawer.

Rhys sidled behind her in the kitchen and massaged her tense shoulders. "You have nothing to be sorry about. I'd rather you be vigilant than complacent."

"I could have stabbed you," she said. Although now that she thought about it, he would have had no problem overpowering her. If he had been the Composer, he could have used her own knife on her. She'd be dead.

"But you didn't." He tucked her hair behind her ear. "Tell me what happened."

Head hanging, she braced her hands on the counter. "I was playing my violin when I heard a noise. It sounded as if it came from one of the bedrooms. I grabbed the knife and planned on running to the deputy's car, but when I opened the door, you were standing there."

He turned her around. There was no recrimination in his expression. All she saw was compassion. "What did the noise sound like?"

"It was a lower-pitched sound, like a thud. Maybe like a door closing or an object hitting the house?"

Rhys pulled his gun from his holster. "Stay here. I'm going to go check it out." His footsteps fell heavy on the wood floor as he strode through the living room to the other side of the house where the bedrooms were located.

She didn't bother arguing. This was his job. She trusted he knew what he was doing. Rhys Keller was born to be an officer of the law. She'd always known it. Back when they were in school, they would sneak to the woods behind the high school at lunch and talk about the future. They had even picked out the land where they'd build their house. Never once had that future involved them living their lives apart.

He had wanted to be sheriff like Griffin had once been. He hadn't approved of Griffin's replacement and planned to one day run against him for the position. It was on those days she almost revealed that she despised Sheriff Pearce as well. But that would have led to questions she didn't want to answer. Rather than divulge her experiences with the sheriff, she'd imagined a future when other people like her in Laurel Creek would have a man in charge who cared more about protecting the community than his reputation.

In all the years they'd been together, Rhys had never mentioned leaving Laurel Creek or joining the FBI, but witnessing him the last couple of days, seeing him in his element, she couldn't picture him doing anything else. She didn't want to admit it to herself, but she was proud of him and what he'd accomplished.

If he hadn't broken up with her, she and Rhys wouldn't be the same people they were today. How many lives had he saved throughout his years in the FBI? While it had been her parents' dream for her she'd ended up living rather than her own, she'd touched thousands of audience members with her music. She couldn't deny her experiences had enriched her life for the better.

Still, she would trade them all to live the life she and Rhys had planned while lying in each other's arms in the woods.

"Julia?" Rhys called out from the other side of the house. "Can you come to the bathroom?"

Dread temporarily glued her feet to the floor. A part of her wanted to remain in the dark and pretend the noise had been her imagination. The other part of her, the part that wasn't a coward, forced the rest of her to walk to the bathroom.

Rhys stood by the window.

The open window.

"Did you open it?" Rhys asked.

She shook her head. "No, and I'm guessing by your question, you didn't either."

He dropped the frosted glass window to the sill,

then lifted it up again, recreating the noise she'd heard.

"That's the thud," she confirmed.

Frowning, he shut the window, locked it, then tried unsuccessfully to lift the glass. "I'm going outside to check something."

She sat on the edge of the bathtub and waited.

A minute later, the window lifted with a thud.

Rhys's irises appeared black as he looked through the empty space where the glass should have been. He strode away, bringing his phone to his ear. "Joshua. The Composer was here. The window in Julia's bathroom has a faulty lock. He was able to open it from the outside. Explains how he got in the first time to steal the music."

Bile climbed up her throat. How many times had he unknowingly invaded her sacred space? All those nights she'd slept in her bed, had he crept inside her home to watch her? After the break-in, the sheriff's office had sworn all her window and door locks functioned correctly. They'd had no explanation for how someone had gotten inside. Even so, she'd hired a locksmith to change the locks on her doors and had double-checked her windows herself to make sure the locks were working. She hadn't thought to check from the outside.

Just knowing the Composer could have hurt her at any time sent literal shivers down her spine. She'd heard the expression, but until now, she'd never experienced it herself.

Mouth dry for the second night in a row, Julia went into the kitchen and poured herself a glass of sweet tea. Thanks to her shaking hands, the liquid sloshed over the sides as she lifted it to her lips.

Yesterday she'd been attacked in her driveway, and now, only twenty-fours later, he'd returned. To do what? Abduct her and kill her like the others? Why her? What had she done to warrant the Composer's wrath? If only she could go back to that moment in time when she'd inspired him to begin writing her letters. If she'd done something differently, played her violin terribly that day or not smiled at him, would none of this have happened? Would those poor women who'd died at the Composer's hand still be alive today? She hated that she asked herself those questions.

She swallowed down the entire glass of tea without taking a breath. If Rhys hadn't arrived when he had, would he have found her dead body on some trail in a couple of days, a tattoo of her music on her naked skin? She closed her eyes as if somehow that would make it all better.

"Hey," Rhys said softly, tugging her toward his chest. "Come here."

It was one thing to rely on him for her physical well-being, but it was another to rely on him for her emotional welfare. She couldn't allow herself to depend on him because it would make it that much harder when they said goodbye to each other again. "You don't need to coddle me. I'll be okay."

He tipped up her chin. "Maybe I'm the one who needs the hug."

Sincerity rang true in his statement. No matter how much it would hurt when he disappeared from her life again, she couldn't deny him. She went willingly into his embrace, burrowing her face into his chest and soaking up his warmth as she clung to him with equal fervor.

His chin rested on the top of her head. "Joshua will make sure the other deputies know to check the perimeter of the house a few times an hour. They're also going to check the window for prints, but I'm not optimistic they'll find anything."

"Does it make me weak to admit I'm terrified?" she said, peeking up at him.

He sifted his fingers through her hair. "It makes you human."

The adrenaline in her system had faded, leaving her exhausted and weak. She felt as if she hadn't slept in days. If Rhys hadn't been holding her, she would've probably collapsed to the floor. While touring and performing was physically demanding, it hadn't prepared her for this kind of stress.

"How do you do this?" she asked him. "How do you deal with violence and death every day?"

"I could say I'm used to it, but that would be a lie. I don't think it's something that anyone gets used to." He clenched his jaw. "Violence is just a part of me. It's who I am."

She laid a palm on his cheek. "That's not true. And that you believe it breaks my heart."

Had he always felt that way? He'd never spoken like that to her before. She knew his mother's murder had affected him. It had affected all of the Keller brothers. But she'd thought it had served to inspire them to become better men. To honor Alicia through religious tradition and to protect society as law enforcement officers. She'd never witnessed this darkness in Rhys before. Had it always been there, lurking beneath his confidence and determination?

A war seemed to be waging behind Rhys's eyes. He wanted to believe her.

His lips parted and his gaze softened. All his muscles went slack as he heaved a sigh.

She thought she'd gotten through to him.

Just like that, the moment was over. With a hardness in his gaze, he took a single step away from her, but the space between them felt as vast as an ocean. "Whoever it was that tried to get in here was pretty bold to do it with a deputy out front. That's why I need to keep a closer eye on you. From here on out, I'm sleeping in your room."

Julia's jaw dropped.

Sleep with Rhys?

Conflicted, she pondered the implications. On one hand, she was relieved. Knowing that the Composer could have gotten into her house whenever he wanted terrified her. A person was never more physically vulnerable than when they slept. Having Rhys beside her with his gun nearby would somewhat reduce her fear. At the same time, sleeping in bed with Rhys made her emotionally vulnerable. It was far more intimate than a hug. Sleeping together, even innocently, would be playing with fire.

She wrung her hands together. "I don't…that is…"

"On the floor," he added, obviously sensing her discomfort. "This isn't a ploy to get you into bed. My one and only concern is keeping you safe."

Everything from the rigidness of his spine to the serious tone of his voice suggested he was telling the truth.

Her body relaxed. "Are you sure you wouldn't rather sleep in the other room or on the couch? The floor won't be very comfortable."

He shook his head. "I'll be fine. Believe me, working for the FBI, I've slept in conditions much worse. Besides, I can't get too comfortable anyway. I need to stay alert in case the Composer gets past the guard outside and tries to break into the house again."

She shivered. "Okay. I'll get you some extra linens to make it a little more comfortable."

Rhys opened his mouth as if he was about to argue, but then quickly shut it. He nodded once. "Thank you, Julia."

She got ready for bed, changing into a T-shirt and shorts and brushing her teeth. After Rhys made some phone calls and spoke with the deputy out front, he covered the window with thick packing tape. It wouldn't work long-term, but it was good enough for tonight.

Julia grabbed two folded comforters from the linen closet and placed them on her bedroom's hardwood floor, creating a padding for Rhys to sleep on. Then she threw a sheet and another comforter on top of it before adding two pillows for his head. There was no way he'd be comfortable, but it was the best she could do.

It was silly. The thought of Rhys watching over her as she slept had a horde of butterflies fluttering around in her belly. He was only doing his job. There was nothing personal about it. He would do this for anyone.

Her heart thumped against her chest as she slipped under her covers and opened her book. She hadn't gotten five pages into it when Rhys, wearing a pair of navy sweatpants and a white T-shirt, appeared in her doorway with his gun in his hand.

He stopped just inside her room. "Can I turn out the lights?"

"Yes, of course." She put her book on the nightstand and reclined, resting her head on the pillow.

Once it was dark, she listened to the rustling sounds of Rhys situating himself beneath the covers she'd left for him on the floor.

Several minutes of silence passed, but she couldn't relax. She felt as if she was holding her breath, waiting for something bad to happen.

Rhys must have sensed she was still awake. "You

know, this is only the second time we've slept together," he said.

She frowned, thinking about the past. He was
right. The only time they'd slept beside each other
had been in a sleeping bag in the mountains. Before
that, they'd slept in different tents with his brothers as chaperones. "I wouldn't call this sleeping together. It's not as if we're sleeping in the same bed."
Her cheeks heated as the words left her lips. "You
said it yourself—you're just doing your job. As soon
as you capture the Composer, things will go back
to normal."

Now that her eyes had adjusted to the darkness,
she could see him positioned on his side, facing her.
"Maybe they don't have to."

A long-forgotten ache bloomed low in her belly.
She couldn't ignore the magnetic pull between them
still existed or that she wanted him just as much—if
not more—as she had back then.

They had avoided having the conversation about
what had broken them up twelve years ago. She
couldn't pretend he hadn't destroyed her. Until they
resolved what had led to his actions after they'd spent
a beautiful day by the waterfall, she couldn't trust
him with her heart. The glue holding the pieces of
it together was too fragile. It wouldn't take much
for him to shatter it all over again. But that didn't
mean she didn't want to try. And if he was feeling
the same? Could he finally get over what had torn
them apart in the first place?

Eager to know what he was thinking, she moistened her lips and turned over on her side to mirror him. "What do you mean?"

He was quiet for a long time. "We were friends first. We can be friends again."

Disappointment crushed her chest. She should have known not to get her hopes up.

"Sure." She faked a smile and turned away from him. "Friends."

He was still the boy who had spent a day by the waterfall planning the future with her and had told her he didn't love her that night.

Nothing had changed.

And it never would.

Chapter Seven

As the sunshine streaming through the window hit Julia like a spotlight, Rhys watched her sleep. Hands tucked under her cheek and her breathing even, Julia looked at peace for the first time in two days. It had taken her hours to fall asleep. He would know, since he hadn't closed his eyes all night. With the Composer's actions growing more reckless, attempting to break in with the deputy outside, Rhys didn't want to take his gaze off Julia for a second. If he hadn't known her life was in danger before, last night had confirmed his suspicion that the Composer intended on making Julia one of his victims.

But that hadn't been the only reason Rhys hadn't slept.

Last night had been an exercise in torture. His torture. He'd almost messed up and asked for another chance before reason returned.

Remembering just how sweet she used to taste and how responsive she had been to his touch, he'd come *this* close to chucking his restraint out the window and telling her he wanted another chance with her. He'd temporarily forgotten all the reasons he'd sent her away from him in the first place.

It had always been that way with her. Whenever they were together, the darkness inside of him went quiet. For a while, he could pretend it didn't exist, that violence didn't lurk beneath his skin. But it did. He was drawn to it like a moth to a flame. And the violence was drawn to him. It was drawn to all the Kellers, no matter how hard they tried to outrun it. Rhys had made peace with that fact the night he had lied to Julia in order to chase her to Europe.

While Sam had cautioned Rhys about turning into their father, he was no different. Neither was Joshua. Like Rhys, his brothers didn't go on dates or own a home or make plans for their future. While it had remained an unspoken agreement, none of them wanted to doom anyone else to their destinies.

But last night, lying on the floor with only feet between them, he had almost crossed a line he could never come back from. Luckily, he'd come to his senses before doing what he'd wanted to do the second he'd stepped into her bedroom—peel their clothes off and remind themselves of how good they used to be together.

He suspected she'd been thinking along the same lines. When she'd accepted his offer of friendship, he could tell by the tone of her voice that he'd hurt her feelings. He hated to do it. But what other choice did he have? Nothing had changed. If anything, a romantic relationship would be even more complicated now that she was in danger. Because danger was his daily reality. He couldn't drag her into it. Once he caught the Composer, she could return to a world free of death and violence—and Rhys.

He frowned as there was a knock on the door. A glance at the clock told him it was only seven in the morning. Who would stop by her house this early?

The second he got to his feet, Julia's head popped up from the pillow.

"Rhys?" she asked, her voice thick with drowsiness.

"Someone's at the door. I'll get it. You go back to sleep." He strode to the door.

Whoever it was better have a good reason for being there that early.

He checked the door's peephole, annoyed to see Joshua's ugly mug on Julia's front porch. He swung open the door. "It's seven in the morning. Julia is still sleeping. What are you doing here?"

"Sorry to come by so early, but I had some news I thought you'd want to know and I wanted to tell you in person." He raised a brown bag. "But I did bring bagels."

Rhys eyed the brown paper bag with interest. "Cream cheese?"

"Of course."

Rhys snatched the bag from Joshua's hand. "Come inside and fill me in."

Joshua's eyes were bloodshot. He'd probably been

working all night. "Owen Baker, Diana Crain's boy-friend, worked as a janitor at the high school at the same time you and Julia attended."

Interesting, but not enough to warrant an early visit. "Okay. I don't see how—"

"You didn't let me finish," Joshua said. "Owen Baker also worked as a janitor at the symphony at the same time."

Wearing a robe, Julia strolled into the room. "I remember Owen. He was nice. He used to give me candy. What about him?"

Rhys put the bag of bagels down on the coffee table and met Julia in front of the couch. He would have preferred to have kept this information from Julia until it became necessary, but Joshua's big mouth had left him no choice. "The reason I left your rehearsal yesterday was because Joshua called me. A woman named Diana Crain went missing two months ago. Her body was found yesterday in the woods behind the high school. Owen and Diana had been dating. He's disappeared."

Her eyes narrowed. "I can't imagine him being the one who stalked me, let alone being responsible for all the murders. I barely knew him."

"Well, he's got a record for assault," Joshua said, "and Diana's mother said her daughter was going to break up with him because, and I quote, 'he scared her.' Among other reasons, Mr. and Mrs. Crain weren't thrilled that Owen was almost two decades older than Diana."

"When was the last time anyone saw him?" Rhys asked.

"A month ago. His current employer, a private janitorial company, told us he just didn't show up for work one day. No notice and no phone call. They actually called the sheriff's office to have us do a welfare check. There was no sign of him at his house."

"Was he questioned in her disappearance?" Julia asked.

Joshua nodded. "He claimed he was home sleeping when she went missing. I know Pearce told you we were close to an arrest, but honestly, we have no physical evidence tying Baker to Diana's death. And the guy had seemed pretty distraught over her disappearance."

"Wouldn't be the first person to fake some tears to throw the police off his scent," Rhys said.

Julia sat on the couch, her skin a tad paler than it had been a few minutes ago. He could tell this was a lot for her to process.

"True," Joshua said. "Anyway, I thought you might want to stop by Baker's house and take a walk around. You know, to check things out. See if there was anything my office missed. I'd go with you, but Pearce has me on a tight leash right now. I'll follow up on that other lead for you today."

With everything that had happened last night, he'd forgotten to fill her in on Lewis Vogel. "Let me take Julia to work and see if Daniel Fenske remembers

Baker, and then I'll head over to his residence. Text me the address."

Julia stayed quiet, her lips pressed together in a thin line as Rhys showed Joshua to the door. Rhys had the feeling her anger was over more than just his failure to communicate the news of the case. She was upset about the mixed messages he'd given her last night. And she had every reason.

The second they were alone, she jumped up from the couch to confront him. "Were you going to tell me about the murder, or were you going to let me find out from the news?"

Defensive, he folded his arms across his chest. "We're not even sure Diana's death has anything to do with the Composer. If I told you about every dead body I saw, you'd have nightmares for weeks. It's better for your sake if you're on a need-to-know basis."

She lifted her chin and planted a hand on her hip. "Then, is there anything else I need to know?"

"Not sure if you noticed, but Lewis Vogel was wearing a bandage on his hand."

"So?" she asked, not making the connection.

"So, I overheard him complaining about you to a couple of the other symphony members. He's not happy you're back."

She rolled her eyes. "Lewis is never happy."

"Well, he injured his hand the same night you scratched your attacker. And he doesn't have an alibi. Joshua is going to bring him in for questioning."

Irritation flashed in her eyes. "How could you not tell me any of this? Don't I deserve to know?"

"Deserve to know? Maybe. Going to know? No. You're not FBI or a cop. You're just a witness," he said, trying to make it clear to her where they stood.

Problem was…they both knew he was lying.

To say that things were frosty between Rhys and Julia the rest of the morning was putting it mildly. Julia had stayed quiet as they headed to the symphony, responding to Rhys's questions by using the least number of words possible. She would barely even look at him.

And it bothered him.

Even when he and Julia had argued as teens—and they'd argued plenty—she'd never shut him out. Either she would have raised her voice, thrown her arms up in the air and fought for what she believed in, or she would have decided to let things go and apologized for her part in the argument. She'd never just frozen him out.

He didn't like it.

Not one bit.

Maybe it was who she was now. They weren't the same people they were a decade ago. The old Julia had had faith in him. He'd been worth fighting for and against. This quietness signified the loss of that faith. She'd given up on him. On them.

That's what he'd wanted, wasn't it? So, why did it bother him so much?

Rhys stayed to watch the beginning of rehearsal.

There were about eighty members of the symphony on that stage, but Julia was the only one he saw. Even as part of a cohesive group, she stood out to him. When she brought the instrument to her chin and slid the bow across the strings, she positively glowed. Unlike most of the others, she didn't have to follow the notes on the page. Her lids drifted shut as she allowed the music to flow through her. It was as if she had become one with it. There was so much joy on her face. She used to wear that joy all the time, but this was the first time he'd seen it since they'd reconnected.

Had he done that to her? Had he stolen that joy?

He used to give her a reason to smile.

He wanted to do it again.

During rehearsal break, Rhys pulled Daniel aside to question him.

"Owen Baker?" Daniel frowned, shuffling sheet music on his podium. "Yes, I remember him. He worked here for about three years."

"Any problems?"

"He was a hard worker." Daniel's hands stilled. He looked up at Rhys. "But I did have to speak with him a couple of times about acting inappropriately toward my younger students."

"Inappropriately?"

Daniel crossed his arms and tilted his face up. "Nothing overt. He had a particular fondness for children. Gave them candy and made silly faces at them during their music lessons. His behavior distracted my students during practice."

Rhys wouldn't exactly call that behavior inappropriate, but for someone like Daniel whose job was to train some of the best juvenile musicians in the country, Rhys could understand why he'd find any distraction inappropriate. "Did Baker have any inappropriate interactions with Julia that you can recall?"

Daniel shook his head, then stopped. "Now that you mention it, there was one time I found him rifling through her backpack. When I confronted him about it, he claimed he'd knocked it over by accident and was just returning the spilled contents."

"You didn't believe him?"

"Julia wouldn't have left her backpack sitting around unzipped. After that, I kept a closer eye on him. I often noticed him watching her as she rehearsed. It bothered me, but there was nothing concrete. Anyway, he eventually found another job, and I forgot all about it."

The backpack thing was odd, but that Daniel had been disturbed by Baker's interest in Julia struck Rhys as significant. "I don't suppose you remember when he stopped working here?"

"Let me think…" Daniel rubbed his chin with his thumb. "Summer. Twelve years ago. I remember because he quit a week before the season's opening concert."

Rhys's gaze wandered to the stage.

Owen Baker had quit working at the symphony when Julia had left for Europe.

Rhys needed to question Baker.

But first, he had to find him.

Chapter Eight

Parking on the side of the dirt road, Rhys got his first glimpse of Owen Baker's home, a well-maintained manufactured house located on the edge of town in Laurel Creek's largest unofficial mobile home park. Unofficial because local zoning laws prohibited them within Laurel Creek.

To get around it, the two-street neighborhood's residents had gotten creative. Unlike a traditional mobile home park, where residents often leased the land, they each owned theirs. It still had cost them more than they could afford, but because they were technically located in unincorporated Laurel Creek, they relied on the county rather than the city for their services, making the cost of land cheaper by several hundred thousand dollars.

The people who lived there worked hourly jobs in town and couldn't afford the astronomical prices demanded elsewhere within Laurel Creek. While there were advantages to the small town being a tourist attraction, affordable housing was not one of them.

Down the road, a few boys rode their bikes in circles, watching him with curiosity. It was clear to Rhys the community looked out for one another. The sight brought back memories of simpler times, when he and his brothers had ridden their bikes into town for ice cream and splashed in the river until nightfall.

Judging by the length of grass in Baker's yard, he hadn't been home to mow it for several weeks. There was a colorful garden in front of the house with purple and yellow daisy-looking flowers interspersed with overgrown green weeds. Someone had taken the time to plant those flowers. Had it been Owen Baker or possibly Diana Crain? The weeds indicated no one had tended to the garden in a while.

There was no sign that anyone was home. No cars out front. A shade covered the window. To the right of the door was a vertical pane of glass. Rhys walked across the grass to get a look inside the home. Passing the garden, he noticed the soil held a reddish tint to it. His evidence collection kit was in the trunk of his car. Before he left, he'd make sure to gather a sample for forensics to compare to the foreign red soil Rhys had found at the crime scene a couple nights ago.

Rhys peeked through the window. There was no movement inside. Joshua had reported that the sheriff's office had already done a sweep of the home when they'd done a welfare check. There was no suggestion a crime had been committed there or anything unusual. Pearce believed Owen had left of his own volition based on the lack of toothbrush in his bathroom and some empty hangers in his closet. But in Rhys's experience, that in itself wasn't conclusive evidence. If someone had abducted or otherwise harmed Owen, it wouldn't be difficult to take a few things to make it look as if Owen left willingly.

Rhys wished more than anything that Julia wasn't entangled in this case. But he couldn't argue she was the lead he needed to solve it. With the stalker's letter now in Rhys's possession, he could match the handwriting of each of the suspects to it. Even if it wasn't obvious, there were experts within the FBI who would be qualified to do so. It was possible her stalker wasn't the Composer, but Rhys's gut said they were one and the same. He was so close to finding the serial killer, he could almost taste it.

A *chirp* came from the back of the house. Rhys's hand went automatically to his holster. The noise sounded like the one a cell phone made with the arrival of a new email or message.

Someone was in the backyard.

Knowing it could be a neighbor or even a kid, Rhys left his gun where it was, but if necessary, he was also prepared to use it. He rounded the corner of the house. The laughter of a child floated in the air. Sweat beaded on his forehead as he trotted toward the back of the home. From his position, he saw the door to an aluminum garden shed in the backyard was wide open.

Had Baker returned home?

Clearing the edge of the house, Rhys went to retrieve his gun. He sensed a presence behind him only a second before he heard the swish of a weapon cutting through the air and the blunt force hit the back of his skull. It was as if a million white lights flared behind his eyes all at once.

Everything went black as he fell to the grass.

Then he didn't sense anything at all.

FINISHED WITH REHEARSAL, Julia returned her violin to its case. It was easy to forget about all her problems when she was focused on her music. Playing the violin was like meditation for her. She fell into a trancelike state where nothing else existed but music. But as soon as she stopped, the chaos of her life returned with a vengeance. Unfortunately, she had decisions to make, and those decisions affected more than just her.

Julia didn't have many friends, and the ones she did have she wasn't close to. She had people to share a meal with or to attend an opera with, but no one to discuss her feelings. Since leaving the town of Laurel Creek and the Kellers, she'd kept her emotions bottled up tight as a drum. The only way she could channel them was through music, especially her own compositions.

Seven years ago, she'd begun composing on a whim when she was stuck in bed with the flu. The pressure for her to perform had been coming from all sides. Her parents. Her manager. The press. Everyone relying on her to entertain the masses for their own personal benefit. There was no one to look out for her. No one not on her payroll to run to the store for medicine and juice. And no one to cry to about it all.

She'd listened to the doctor who'd warned her that performing while sick with the flu could cause her to end up in the hospital with pneumonia. She'd canceled two weeks of concerts and allowed herself to fully recuperate. By that time, she'd been touring for three years without a break. She hadn't had a moment to herself. Four days into her bed rest, she'd grown tired of reading and watching television.

She'd had her assistant bring her some blank sheets and spent the next week notating the music she heard in her head. It was as if she'd been possessed. She'd poured all of her sorrow, her frustration and her loneliness into the pieces. By the time she'd returned to performing, she'd composed three pieces. It took longer to get musicians to play it and even longer to make the corrections. Eventually, she'd grown confident enough to perform them for audiences.

The music world no longer saw her solely as a performer.

She was famous for being a composer as well.

"Waterfall" was her newest composition. She'd spent five years working on it, never quite able to perfect it. The day after moving back to Laurel Creek, she'd finished. The piece represented twelve years of regret and longing for the moments in Laurel Creek she'd spent with Rhys.

Then a serial killer had stolen the sheet music from her home and distorted it for his own sadistic purposes. To Julia, each note embodied the love she and Rhys had shared, but to the Composer's victims, they were markings of their deaths.

For that reason, it seemed inconsiderate—even cruel—to play the piece at their upcoming concert.

She needed advice. And since she refused to discuss anything with Rhys at the moment—she was still furious with him—there was only one person to turn to.

Backstage, Julia walked down the hall toward the symphony offices. Someone was shouting in Daniel's office. Not someone. She recognized the voice. Lewis was yelling at Daniel. She stopped, torn between whether to stay and listen or to turn around and go back to the auditorium. It wasn't as if she were eavesdropping. Lewis wasn't attempting to be quiet. Anyone and everyone in the office area could hear him. Still, it would be rude to stand in the hallway and listen. She swiveled on her heels when she heard her name mentioned, as well as the derogatory term he attributed to her.

Rhys had mentioned Lewis's dislike of her, but she hadn't realized the extent of it. He didn't merely dislike her. He hated her. Venom dripped with every word he uttered. He was threatening to have his parents withdraw financial support from the Laurel Creek Symphony if Daniel didn't give him first chair.

Lewis was extremely talented but had always been

difficult to work with. His parents were founders of the town and had donated millions of dollars to the symphony. Much more than her parents ever had. Daniel couldn't afford to lose that money.

Daniel murmured a response, but it was too quiet to hear. His office door flew open, smacking the wall, and a red-faced Lewis stormed out. There was nowhere for her to hide.

Lewis's long strides ate up the distance between them before she could escape. He flung her around and smashed her spine against the wall. Wincing from the impact, she didn't want to show fear, but her body hadn't gotten the memo. She felt as if she were a newborn horse, standing on wobbly legs for the first time.

Both hands grabbed her by the collar as he bent his neck to speak in her face. "You think you're special, but you're nothing. You're a second-rate violinist and a mediocre composer. You slept your way to the top, and your parents have helped you stay there. But the public will learn the truth about you soon enough. And when it does, your career will be over. I'll make sure of it. Or you can leave town now and save yourself from what I have planned for you. It's your decision."

As quickly as he'd accosted her, he released her. It had all happened within seconds, but it felt as if it had lasted hours. Her heart pounded wildly, making her dizzy, and her knees buckled. Shaking, she slumped against the wall, using the plaster to keep her upright as he disappeared around the corner.

What had he meant by all that? Was it simply an empty threat, or did he really have something planned? She'd known he was a spoiled brat and that he typically acted with disdain toward everyone, but to her knowledge, he'd never acted violently. Was he capable of murder? Before, she would've said no, but after displaying that kind of rage, she believed differently.

Daniel came running out of his office. "Julia, are you okay? Was that Lewis yelling at you?"

She let out a shuttered breath. "Yes, it was Lewis, but I'm fine. He didn't hurt me," she said weakly. Had he always had a temper like that? There was a monster lurking inside of Lewis Vogel. How had she never known?

While Lewis's behavior had terrified her, he hadn't left any marks on her, and no one had witnessed the incident. It would be her word against his, and the sheriff had already made it clear he thought she was a liar.

"I'm so sorry you heard all that." Daniel sighed. "Lewis has these tantrums now and then. It's best to let him get it out rather than to engage him in a battle of wills. I've ignored it over the years, but it's inexcusable for him to behave that way toward you or any other member of the symphony. I think it's time for the symphony and Lewis Vogel to part ways."

"No," she said vehemently. "You can't do that. I

heard him threaten to pull his parents' funding." As much as it scared her to work with Lewis, his family's money was vital to the survival of the symphony. She didn't want to be reason for the symphony's loss of income.

Daniel waved it off. "It would hurt the symphony temporarily, but we'll survive. There are other donors out there."

They were brave words, but they were also a lie. There was only one reason Daniel had tolerated Lewis's behavior all these years, and that reason was he had no other choice.

Back in the 1940s, Lewis's grandparents had paid for the property's conversion from a church to a symphony hall. They, along with two other families, were responsible for saving the entire town from financial ruin after the area's gem mines dried up. Lewis wasn't the only Vogel to benefit from his family name. The Vogels' financial lending company held the mortgages of over half the properties in town, both businesses and homes. The other families were equally as prominent in the community, its members holding high-level positions, such as the town's mayor and financial manager.

Daniel couldn't afford to take on Lewis and his family. The symphony would never survive it.

Having regained her composure, Julia stepped away from the wall. "The Vogels have too much power in Laurel Creek. If Lewis is thrown out of the symphony, what's to keep them from having their

friends withdraw their donations too? Don't do anything drastic. Being first chair isn't important to me.
Let Lewis have it."

"He doesn't deserve it. You do."

She gave him a small smile. "Maybe, but my pride
isn't contingent on it."

Daniel placed a hand on her shoulder. "You are
the most compassionate person I know. I'm so proud
of you."

Her chest filled with warmth. "Thank you." After
everything he'd done for her, she was happy to make
his life a little easier. "I was actually hoping I could
talk to you. Do you have a couple of minutes?"

"For you? Always." He gestured for her to follow him down the hall. "Come into my office, and
we'll chat."

Daniel sat behind his desk, and she settled onto
the cushioned chair on the other side from him. Now
that she had a moment to really look at him, she saw
how tired he appeared. The whites of his eyes were
bloodshot, and purplish crescent-shaped bags swelled
underneath. Had he been getting enough sleep?

She couldn't help feeling responsible for some of
his exhaustion. "I'm sorry my coming back here has
made such a mess for you."

"Nonsense," he said firmly. "Your parents made
you believe you're a burden, but their loss was my
gain. I don't have any family of my own, which is
why I always regarded you as a daughter."

"You never talk about them." She relaxed and

crossed her legs. In all these years, he hadn't mentioned anything about his family other than to tell her they were dead. She'd always been curious about them though. Her parents had been thrilled to convince Daniel to take her on as his student. He had apparently been some kind of child musical prodigy, but he'd never spoken about it.

There were times it would have been good to have someone who understood what it was like for her. Unfortunately, despite his claim to regard her as a daughter, he'd always kept a professional distance between them and rarely shared anything personal. Privacy was something he valued highly, which was why it had been nearly impossible to find anything about his younger self on the internet and only a few items on him as an adult. He didn't give interviews or pose for photos.

Sometimes, she wished she'd followed his example.

"My mother was a musician," Daniel said, surprising her. "She died from cancer when I was ten."

"I'm sorry."

"I loved her very much, but it was a long time ago. You remind me so much of her. You even have the same blond hair. She was incredibly gifted and exceedingly kind. Like me, she played several instruments." Sadness lingered in his eyes. "If she had lived another kind of life, she would have been a star, like you. But that wasn't in the cards for her. Still, her love of music lives on in me and all of those I've been privileged to teach, including you."

Her throat thickened with compassion for his loss. Julia was so fortunate to have him in her life. "I feel like I haven't thanked you enough for everything you've done for me throughout the years. I know my parents donated a substantial amount of money to the symphony and paid you for my lessons, but you went above and beyond for me." They probably didn't give as much as the Vogels, but it was considerable. Part of the reason he'd been promoted to conductor of the Laurel Creek Symphony was due to the donations he'd brought in. "There were times I resented you because of it," she said.

"I know. You missed your parents." He interlinked his hands, resting his arms on the desk. "Julia, while I'm thrilled to have you back home, I can't help but think you'd be safer if you postponed your first concert. Maybe left town for a bit until the Composer is caught."

She chuckled. If he wanted her to leave town, she assumed he wouldn't want her playing "Waterfall" in the concert. "You sound like Rhys."

"He's a smart man. I was always fond of him. At least, that is, until he broke your heart." Daniel gave her a pointed look. "I'm concerned he's going to do it again."

"I won't let him. I'm a grown woman now and my eyes are wide open." Especially after sending her all those mixed signals. She hadn't imagined the tension between them in bed last night. He had wanted to kiss her.

"I'm not sure it's as easy as that. You still love him, don't you?" Daniel asked, getting to the heart of the matter.

"It's irrelevant. Love was never our problem." To keep her hands busy, she picked up a paper clip from the desk and went to work on straightening the metal. "The reasons we broke up haven't changed."

That comment he'd made about things not having to return to normal? She could have sworn he'd been implying they'd have a romantic relationship. But over the next eight hours, she'd gone from being a "friend" to just a "witness" in his case. Something had spooked him, and it was the same thing that had spooked him all those years ago.

"What does Rhys think about you staying in Laurel Creek with a killer on the loose?" Daniel asked.

"He doesn't like it, but we came to an understanding." She concentrated her attention on the paper clip. "He's staying at my house."

"Are you sure that's wise?"

She lifted a shoulder. "Wise? No. Necessary? Yes."

"Do your parents know what's going on here?"

"No." She could only imagine how they'd respond. "They weren't pleased I left the opportunity of a lifetime to come back to what they refer to as 'that Podunk town.' To them, my decision was a late-stage act of defiance directed at them. If they found out about the Composer, you know as well as I do they'd use it as an excuse to convince me to return to Europe."

She could count on one hand how many times she'd seen them in the past five years. They didn't care about her. Through genetics, they'd created a musical prodigy. She represented an achievement to them. *Their achievement.* But they didn't deserve the credit.

"You know what they wouldn't do?" She leaned forward. "They wouldn't cancel one of their concerts to fly to Georgia and make sure I was safe. They wouldn't make a cup of tea and sit down with me to discuss their concerns. They've never been the ones I've turned to. You're more my father than my dad ever was."

He placed a hand over his heart. "I'm honored."

"If I run back to Europe, then the Composer wins, and I'm not going to let one more person dictate how to live my life," Julia said. "Laurel Creek is my home and I'm not leaving. If that means I have to live with the man who broke my heart, then that's what I'm going to do."

It turned out, she didn't need Daniel's advice after all. She'd made her decision.

She stood, determination coursing through her veins. "Because come Sunday evening, as scheduled, I will premiere 'Waterfall' at the opening concert of the season. I won't allow anyone to stop me—not even the Composer."

RHYS WOKE SLOWLY, as if he were a computer booting up after its battery had died. *What happened?* For just a split second, he couldn't remember where he was or what he'd been doing.

His senses came back to him piecemeal. His head throbbed. He smelled grass and dirt. He heard a lawn mower in the distance. The sun was beating on the back of his neck. He was lying facedown.

He tried opening his eyes, but nausea forced him to close them again. Rolling over, he moaned involuntarily, dizzy from the action.

"Easy, son," said a familiar voice. "You've got a nasty bump building on the back of your skull."

The first thing Rhys saw when he opened his eyes was Sheriff Pearce standing over him. "How long have I been out?"

"Don't know. Just got here a second ago." Pearce glanced at the watch on his wrist. "But it's a few minutes after eleven if that helps."

That meant he'd only been unconscious for a minute or two. *When had the sheriff gotten there?*

Rhys squinted up at Pearce, blinded by the sun. "You didn't happen to see anyone running around with a bat or anything, did you?"

"Someone hit you with a bat?"

"Bat. Crowbar." He hadn't seen the weapon or the person who attacked him. "Hit me with something solid enough to knock me out."

"Probably just got you in the right spot." The sheriff offered a hand, and a dizzy Rhys would be an idiot if he didn't accept it. "I doubt you'd be talking right now if you were hit with a bat."

"Good to know." Once he was on his feet, Rhys reached around and felt the lump on his head. When his hand came back bloody, he coughed, gagging. He had no trouble seeing other people's blood but couldn't stand to see his own. "What are you doing here?"

Sheriff Pearce's appearance there seemed too coincidental, and his timing was awfully convenient. He'd surfaced a couple minutes after Rhys's assault but had managed to miss Rhys's attacker.

"I'm guessing the same as you. Checking to see if Baker came home."

It was a plausible excuse. Pearce had a legitimate reason to be there. Still, Rhys didn't trust him. The sheriff had made it clear he resented the FBI's intrusion into what he considered local matters. He'd accused Julia of lying about her stalker and had minimized both her attack and the burglary. What if Sheriff Pearce's reluctance to believe Julia had nothing to do with negligence? What if he had a more personal reason?

Had he been the one to hit Rhys in the back of the head? Had Rhys stumbled onto something the sheriff wanted to keep hidden?

But if he'd been the one to knock Rhys out, where'd the weapon go?

Rhys glanced at the backyard, immediately spotting the difference from earlier. "The shed door was open."

"Closed now," Sheriff Pearce said, pointing out the obvious. "I thought I told you to lay off the Crain murder."

"Actually, you told me the coroner hadn't determined cause of death yet." It didn't skip Rhys's attention that Pearce had quickly changed the subject rather than following up on Rhys's observation. Was that because he already knew who'd shut the shed door?

"It was homicide. Asphyxiation. Bruising suggests he beat her up first, then put a garbage bag over her head to kill her. No sign of fingerprints yet, but forensics will keep looking."

The Composer hadn't beaten his victims. He'd used a drug to subdue them. But if it had been a crime of opportunity, and something had set him off—like hearing Julia was returning to Laurel Creek—he would've been angry enough to use his fists.

Maybe they'd get lucky.

In an unplanned crime, a suspect was more likely to mess up and leave evidence behind.

"So, you're in agreement Diana Crain's murder is related to the Composer?" Rhys asked, surprised the sheriff was willing to share information with him.

"I'm not ruling it out." The sheriff turned and walked away, saying over his shoulder, "You should go to the hospital and get your head examined."

Rhys stood there, stunned. "Was that a joke?"

The sheriff didn't respond.

Maybe Pearce wasn't as bad as he seemed.

Or maybe he was worse.

Chapter Nine

Julia took the last bite of the salmon she'd prepared for dinner and pushed the plate away. She hadn't heard from Rhys all day. It had taken several hours, but her ire toward him had cooled considerably. Rhys hadn't hurt her deliberately. He always had her best interests in mind, even when he was acting like an idiot. Whether they were friends or something more, they were temporarily living together. Arguments were inevitable.

It had been years since she'd had any kind of personal relationship that required two-way communication, and although they hadn't discussed it, she got the sense Rhys hadn't either. She'd chastised him for keeping her in the dark about the case, but hadn't she done the same by failing to tell him about her stalker?

They both had their secrets and scars.

Maybe it wasn't fair of her to expect more of him.

She carried her empty plate to the sink and placed Rhys's full plate on the counter. As an apology for her part in their argument, she'd made dinner for him. She scrubbed the dirty dishes until they sparkled, and after covering Rhys's dinner with plastic wrap, she set it in the refrigerator for him. At this point, she wasn't even sure he'd be coming home.

He hadn't returned any of her messages.

The lock of the front door engaged with a *snick*.

Her excitement over seeing Rhys was dulled by the sight of him holding an ice pack to the back of his head. There were dark shadows under his eyes, and his skin was pale.

He was injured.

She instinctively rushed toward him. "What happened? Are you okay?"

He gave her a little smile, but she could tell it was forced. "Just a little bump on the head. My brothers have done worse. Don't worry about me."

He wasn't kidding about his brothers. She couldn't count how many times he'd sported a bruise somewhere on his body given to him by Sam or Joshua during a friendly game of football or some other so-called fun activity.

"Did you at least get it checked out by a doctor? What if you have a concussion?"

"Wouldn't be the first time. Besides, I went to the hospital. I have a mild concussion, but after they did a couple tests, they confirmed there was no intracranial bleeding." His small smile turned into a salacious grin. "But if you're worried, you can wake me up a few times during the night." He raised his eyebrows suggestively, then grimaced, hissing in pain.

She was so relieved to see him that she didn't even care that he'd gone back to making suggestive comments. She hadn't admitted to herself just how much she loved spending time with him. If her behavior this morning had frightened him away, she would've always regretted it.

"How did this happen?" she asked, going behind him to check out his injury. There was a white bandage underneath the ice pack. She poked at it gently, feeling the unnatural lump it covered. That wasn't a little bump on the head. It was massive.

"Someone hit me from behind," he mumbled.

Looked like his pride had also taken a beating. "Who?"

"Unfortunately, I didn't get the chance to ask. I was knocked out for a minute, and when I came to, he was gone."

Should he be standing?

She led him to the couch. "You were knocked unconscious? I can't believe the hospital didn't admit you."

He sagged against the cushions. "They wanted to, but I signed out against doctor's orders. I won't argue if you want to nurse me back to health."

She huffed out a breath in irritation as she settled beside him. "I don't know how you can make jokes about it. You could've died. You should be in the hospital recovering."

Was this what it would have been like to be the wife of an FBI special agent? When they'd planned for their futures all those years ago, she hadn't considered the danger that came with a job in law enforcement. She'd assumed a Laurel Creek deputy sheriff wouldn't see much action. Looking back now, that seemed awfully naive, considering she had been stalked and Alicia had been murdered in that town.

But now, the dangers associated with his job were much greater. He wasn't dealing with small-town crimes. He specialized in serial killers. While she was proud of what he'd accomplished in his career, she also worried about the risks that went along with it.

His eyes closed. "My skull is tougher than it looks."

If only that were true. He was trying to downplay the incident, but he was obviously in pain. She inched closer to him and gently slipped her arm around his neck. "Rhys. Tell me what happened."

He leaned into her, resting his head on her shoulder. "I was checking out Owen Baker's property when I heard a noise in the backyard. I went to check, and someone whacked me in the back of my skull. When I came to, the sheriff was standing over me."

That was creepy. And odd. "Sheriff Pearce? Did he see anything?"

"He claims he didn't," Rhys said in a tone that implied he believed otherwise.

"You think he lied to you?"

He briefly peered up at her before shuttering his eyes again. "I don't trust him."

She didn't trust the sheriff either. He'd never given

her reason to. And that said a lot, because she gave the benefit of the doubt to everyone.

At the same time, she didn't see the sheriff being the type to wallop an FBI special agent over the head. No, he'd have someone else do his dirty work. Still, he'd made it clear he didn't appreciate Rhys's presence in Laurel Creek. She just didn't understand why. In her view, the more people protecting the town's residents, the better. What did it matter if help came from outside the sheriff's office?

Remembering how much Rhys used to enjoy it, Julia caressed her fingers over the top of his scalp to relax him. "Do you trust anyone?"

"I trust my brothers," he said firmly. After a pause, he said, "I trust you."

Did he? She tamped down the flicker of anger his words caused. The last thing they both needed was another argument, especially in Rhys's condition. But if there was any hope for them to have any type of relationship, it was time for them both to be honest with one another. "If you trusted me, you wouldn't keep things from me."

He opened his eyes. "I got your messages and your apology for this morning. I thought that meant you understood there are details of my job I can't divulge."

"I get that." She didn't like it, but she understood there were parts of him he couldn't share. "I was referring to those things that relate to us on a personal level."

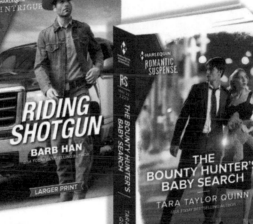

Get up to 4 FREE FABULOUS BOOKS You Love!

To thank you for being a loyal reader we'd like to send you up to 4 FREE BOOKS, absolutely free when you try the Harlequin Reader Service.

Just write "YES" on the Loyal Reader Voucher and we'll send you 2 free books from each series you choose and a Free Mystery Gift, altogether worth over $20.

Try **Harlequin® Romantic Suspense** and get 2 books featuring heart-racing page-turners with unexpected plot twists and irresistible chemistry that will keep you guessing to the very end.

Try **Harlequin Intrigue® Larger-Print** and get 2 books featuring action-packed stories that will keep you on the edge of your seat. Solve the crime and deliver justice at all costs

Or **TRY BOTH and get 2 books from each series!**

Your free books are completely free, even the shipping! If you continue with your subscription, you can look forward to curated monthly shipments of brand-new books from your selected series, always at a discount off the cover price! Plus you can cancel any time.

So don't miss out, return your Loyal Readers Voucher today to get your Free books.

Pam Powers

LOYAL READER
FREE BOOKS VOUCHER

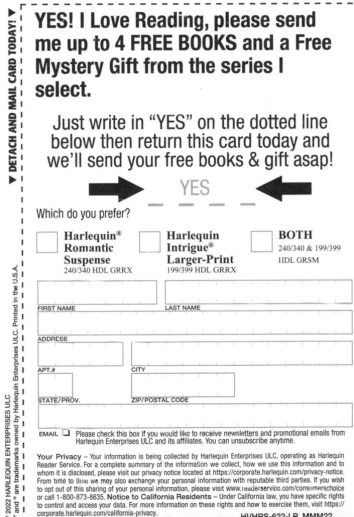

♦HARLEQUIN® Reader Service —Here's how it works:

Rhys raised his head from her shoulder. "What things?"

"How about your propensity for making decisions that are mine to make? You did it after graduation and you're doing it again. You act as if I'm a fragile object that you have to handle with care instead of a grown woman capable of choosing what's best for herself."

He glanced away. "I don't know what you're talking about."

"Yes, you do." She recognized guilt when she saw it. Despite Rhys's effort to hide it, there was a whole bucketful of guilt in his eyes. If Rhys believed he was truly doing what was best for her, then why would he feel guilty over it? She wouldn't be able to move on with her life until she got to the heart of why Rhys was so desperate to keep her at arm's length. "Tell me the truth. I'm more than a witness in a case to you, aren't I?"

She already knew the answer, but she needed to hear him admit to it.

Rhys grew rigid, a tic in his cheek jumping from the clenching of his jaw. He pressed his fingers into the fabric covering his solid thighs. She sensed a conflict raging within him. Why didn't he want her to know the truth? What was so difficult about admitting he cared for her? It wasn't as if she would lord it over him. Ultimately, it had been his choice to end things between them. If she wasn't worth fighting for, there was nothing she could do to change his mind.

"You are," he said, his voice breaking. "You're much more than a witness to me."

His admission confirmed her suspicion. He didn't trust her and never had. "You lied to me."

"I did." He swallowed hard as he took her hand and laced their fingers together. "I had to let you go. I lied so that you wouldn't miss out on the opportunity of a lifetime. I lied because I loved you."

It was as if she had taken her first breath after twelve years of holding it. Even though she'd strongly suspected he'd lied to her, she had needed him to say the words. He had loved her. What they'd shared hadn't been an illusion. She'd thought hearing the truth would set her free and she'd be able to put the past behind her. But instead, she mourned for what they'd both lost.

"I know." At her admission, Rhys jolted, sitting up straight and his eyes widening in shock. She shook her head at him. He hadn't really known her, had he? Maybe that had been her fault. She'd always seen him as her knight in shining armor, so how could she blame him for acting like it? "Don't look so surprised. I may have been young, but I was never as naive as you thought I was."

"But you left for Europe anyway," Rhys said, confusion in his tone.

The night they'd broken up still haunted her. After

all the years that had passed, the emotions lingered in the air, if not the exact words of the conversation.

"Because I deserved better," she said, squaring her shoulders. "You thought my love for you made me weak, as if it were an illness I could recover from with enough time and distance. You might have loved me, but you didn't believe in me. You didn't fight for me. That's why I left." Just like her parents, he'd tossed her aside as if she'd meant nothing to him. What was it about her that made it so easy for people to send her away?

"I always believed in you. That's why I broke up with you. You would have stayed in Laurel Creek if I hadn't."

She jumped up from the couch and threw her hands in the air. "That should have been my decision to make. Not yours." If only he'd chosen to have a conversation about it, their lives would have been completely different.

"If it had been your decision, you wouldn't have left," he said as if that made his actions acceptable.

That wasn't the point. "Maybe, maybe not, but you never even gave me the chance."

Rhys tossed his ice pack onto the coffee table and stood. "You would have given up your dreams for me, and I couldn't allow that to happen."

Her dreams? When he'd broken up with her, he'd popped her dreams like a balloon. In a single night, she'd lost everything she ever wanted. It couldn't have hurt more if he'd physically stabbed her in the

heart. The pain was less intense now, but it still lingered, forever haunting her.

"Don't you understand?" Her voice broke. "Trav-
eling the world, without a real home or a family to fill
it, was never my dream. It was my *parents'* dream.
They were the ones who didn't want to plant roots or
raise the child they'd brought into the world."

She reached out and cradled his face in her hands,
making sure he would hear every word of what she
was about to say. "But my dream was you. It was of
buying that property down the street from your father and designing a home big enough for the family
we'd build together. It was of me as your wife lighting the Sabbath candles at the Friday-night dinners
you have with your brothers. And of teaching music
to kids and sowing the creativity of the next generation of musicians. I dreamed of supporting you in
your career in law enforcement, even though every
time you walked out the door, I'd worry you might
not make it home to me. All those things we talked
about in the woods behind the school and at our spot
by the waterfall. Those were my dreams."

His eyes softened as if he were picturing it all in
his mind. He slipped his hands around her waist to
the small of her back.

Julia stared at his lips, remembering their softness
and the way they'd whisper across her skin as she and
Rhys sunbathed on the rocks beside the waterfall. It
ached to know the most special moments of her life
had been illusions. "I thought they were yours too.

But all of them were just lies, weren't they? You never meant one word of them."

His fingers had found their way under her shirt, the heat of them pressing into her lower spine, drawing her closer to him. "I wanted them to be true. I never lied to you. Not once." He took a deep breath. "Not until I told you I didn't love you."

His admission flowed through her like warm maple syrup. It hadn't all been a lie. He'd loved her once. But he hadn't loved her like she'd loved him. If so, he would have never broken her with such careless disregard. "You might think you loved me, but it wasn't enough for you to fight for me." She hesitated to ask but decided she needed to know the truth. "What is it about me that's so easy to abandon?"

"Easy?" He shook his head. "Letting you go was the hardest thing I've ever done." Before she could respond, his mouth was on hers, stealing the air in her lungs as well as her good sense. He pressed her against him, then plunged his hands in her hair, cradling her head in his palms and taking total control of the kiss.

His taste exploded on her tongue and roused her cells at their most intimate level. Her pulse thrummed a quickened beat that she felt throughout her body. It was as if the earth had tilted on its axis and was spinning like a merry-go-round, making her dizzy and weightless. He nudged her backward until they both fell onto the couch. His warm lips plied hers with expert mastery, obliterating any doubt she had about whether she'd overestimated their chemistry in her mind all these years. If anything, it was more explosive than she'd remembered.

He gently pressed her back into the cushions and covered her body with his. The hardness of him molded to the softness of her. He skated his palm down her rib cage and stopped on her hip. The flexing of his fingers was the only warning she got before Rhys bunched her shirt's hem in his hand and slowly lifted it. In response, she wrapped her feet around his legs and murmured her consent between kisses.

A vibration stretched along the back of her thigh, and a muffled chime sounded from Rhys's pocket. She placed the pads of her fingers at the corner of his lips. "Your phone's ringing," she said into his mouth.

He dropped his head and sighed, his hair tickling her cheek. "I better take this. It's Joshua's ringtone." Sitting up, he brought his phone to his ear. He listened for a minute before lowering his cell to his lap. "There's been a break in the case. The sheriff located Owen Baker. He's at the station being questioned, and Pearce has agreed to hold him there for me."

She stood from the couch. It was good news.

So why was she so disappointed? "That's great."

Rhys grabbed her hand. "I want you to come with me to the station. I've got an idea."

Chapter Ten

Rhys left Julia in the sheriff's office waiting room
with her book and a lukewarm cup of coffee. She'd
been all too delighted to accompany him down to the
station and take a more active role in the investigation, and he preferred she stayed nearby, where Rhys
could keep an eye on her. Not that he didn't trust the
deputies, but they didn't have the innate instinct to
protect her as he did. After their kiss, he could no
longer deny Julia was more than a case witness and
more than a friend. Exactly what she meant to him
remained undefined.

All he knew was that he'd not only kill for her—
he'd die for her too. And it had nothing to do with
his job as a special agent.

Tearing himself away from Julia's lips earlier had
physically pained him. Her flavor still lingered in his
mouth. It had been a long time since one of his brothers had disturbed one of his special moments with
Julia, and he couldn't say he'd missed it. He used to
think they had some kind of detector for knowing

the worst times to interrupt. Now he understood it was sheer dumb luck.

On the ride over, Julia and Rhys had avoided the subject of the kiss. He'd thought about bringing it up, but the timing seemed off. Once Rhys had gotten the call from Joshua, Julia became his witness again. It was difficult to shove her back into that category now that he'd kissed her. His initial annoyance over Joshua's interruption had turned into relief. If that call hadn't happened, without a doubt, Rhys and Julia would have made love. And he wasn't ready to make the commitment that came along with it. Inevitably, he would only hurt her again.

He still hadn't told her the complete truth about why he'd ended things all those years ago. How could he explain that a life spent with him meant a lifetime of violence? He didn't want that for her. If he had told her the truth, she'd insist it was her decision to make, just as she'd insisted last night. He would want to believe her. But there were worse things than breaking her heart. His father had learned that lesson the hard way.

Rhys eyed Pearce with growing suspicion. It hadn't been the sheriff who'd suggested contacting Rhys about Baker's presence at the station. Joshua had taken it upon himself to make the call. While Pearce hadn't outright objected, it was clear by the sourness of his expression that he wasn't pleased to have Rhys there. Odd, because in Baker's yard, the sheriff had shared Diana Crain's cause of death.

A nervous Baker bounced his knees underneath the table, causing the whole thing to shake. Deputy Matt Levy, one of Rhys's friends from synagogue, had been off doing some shopping at the Laurel Creek Home Improvement Store when he'd caught Baker purchasing some rope, zip ties and a shovel. Once word got to Pearce, the sheriff arrived to personally arrest Baker for the misdemeanor of hindering law enforcement activity. Surprisingly, Baker had waived his right to an attorney, which was a stupid move. But it wasn't Rhys's call to make, and it sure would make his job an easier one.

Sitting next to Rhys, Joshua had agreed to let him have first crack at Baker. Pearce was busy outside the station giving a press conference.

After reciting Baker's rights for the purpose of the recording, Rhys reclined in his chair and crossed his legs, trying to display a casualness that Baker would perceive as nonthreatening. "Where've you been, Owen? People have been looking for you all month. You've got to admit your disappearance didn't look good. Guy with a missing girlfriend suddenly disappears without a trace a month after her disappearance."

In his late thirties, Baker had a baby face that made him appear a decade younger. He was wearing a tattered muscle shirt, ripped jeans and an Atlanta Braves baseball cap over his shaggy mullet of white-blond hair. "I already told Sheriff Pearce, I went to the mountains. There were no leads here in

Laurel Creek, and Pearce wasn't doing anything new to solve the case. In his view, the investigation into Di's disappearance was a waste of taxpayer money. They'd already stopped talking about her case on the news. I had to do something other than put up flyers around town."

If Baker's frustration with the progress in the investigation was real, Rhys could understand it. He didn't doubt Joshua's department had done everything they could to find her, but when leads went cold, their hands were tied. "Why the mountains?"

Baker's gaze shifted to the corner of the room. "I heard about those girls that were found on the trails. I thought maybe that same guy or some other maniac kidnapped her and was holding her in a cabin somewhere in the mountains. I don't know." He shrugged. "Sounds stupid when I say it out loud. I just couldn't sit around anymore and do nothing."

Something Baker had said was a lie. Exactly what he'd lied about, Rhys didn't know. *The reason he went to the mountains?*

"Why didn't you tell anyone where you were going?" Rhys asked, keeping confrontation out of his voice.

Tilting his head, Baker looked right at Rhys. "There was no one to tell. I don't speak to my family, and my friends aren't exactly the type you call when you need help."

"What about the National Park Service or one of the ranger stations? Did you check in with them to let them know you were there? Write your information with the date and where you were going into the notebook at the trail's entrance?" It was an archaic system, but hikers disappeared on the trails all the time, and the notebooks often helped to locate them.

"Nah, I wasn't worried about anything happening to me." Baker tapped his fingers on the table. "I only cared about finding Di."

Joshua leaned forward in his chair. "I'm curious. If you were there in the mountains for a month with no one around and no one to vouch for you, how did you know if Diana was still missing?"

Baker paused a beat too long. "I checked the news on my cell."

"You didn't come back to town at all during the month?" Rhys asked.

"No." Again Baker's gaze darted away, revealing his lie.

"You must have known the sheriff's office would want to speak with you again," Joshua said.

Baker's lips twisted into a sneer. "Well, your boss told me Diana had probably left town and not bothered to tell anyone. But Diana wouldn't do that. He didn't know her. She had anxiety disorder. Everything had to be just so, or she'd have a panic attack. She probably had one that night."

Rhys's interest sparked. "Tell me more about her panic attacks."

"Di got real nervous from change. One time, the burger joint on Main swapped out the old sesame seed bun with some fancy pretzel roll for their chicken sandwich, and she couldn't eat it. Spent the rest of the night crying on and off about it too. Even when they went back to using their old buns, she wouldn't go back to the restaurant."

"You told me you were supposed to pick up Diana from work the night she disappeared. What happened?" Joshua asked.

"I overslept. I was only a few minutes late. If I had shown up like I said I would, she would still be alive."

"You can't know that," Rhys said. But if her murder had been a crime of opportunity, Baker was right. She'd likely be alive if he'd driven her home as promised.

"I loved her. We'd talked about getting married. I know she was a lot younger, but we just got each other."

The odd thing was Rhys believed him. He still considered Baker a suspect, but he wasn't lying about his feelings for Diana. Love was all too often a strong motivation for murder. On the flip side, if Baker was telling the truth, it was likely Diana had been suffering from a panic attack when she left the store the night she disappeared. She would have been on high alert, anxious of anything else out of the ordinary. But what if someone she knew—someone she trusted— had offered to give her a ride home?

Someone like the sheriff.

For now, it was just a theory, one of many. And it was time to focus on another one.

"What did her parents think about your relationship?" Rhys asked.

Baker rolled his eyes, not even pretending Rhys hadn't poked a sore spot. "They don't like me. They wanted her to date a guy her own age, someone with money. Money meant nothing to her. They didn't understand her. Not like I did."

Rhys smiled at Baker as if they were talking over beers at the bar rather than across the table at the sheriff's department. "Have you always dated young girls, Owen?"

"Diana isn't—wasn't—a young girl." Baker frowned. "She was turning twenty."

"But you've been dating since she was seventeen, right? And you were—what—almost forty?"

"Thirty-five. And it was legal in Georgia," Baker said defensively.

Rhys gave him a sly grin. "Have you dated anyone else younger than seventeen?"

Baker started to speak, then stopped himself. He narrowed his eyes. "What if I have? What does that have to do with anything?"

Since Baker had seen through Rhys's good-guy act, he might as well get straight to the point. "Did you ever want to date Julia Harcourt?"

"Julia Harcourt?" Baker removed his hat and scratched his scalp. "Who…the violinist? Haven't heard that name in years."

Rhys assessed Baker's reaction. He couldn't tell if it was sincere. "What do you remember about her?"

"I don't know. It's been, like, what, a freakin' decade?" Baker plopped his cap back on his head. "She was talented. That's for sure. But I felt bad for her, you know? That music teacher guy worked her to the bone. He was really strict. Expected all those kids to practice for hours, so I'd act goofy and try to make them laugh. Feed them candy during a break. Anything to get them to smile and enjoy themselves. Julia especially needed it the most."

For a man who'd initially purported not to remember Julia, he sure remembered a heck of a lot now. "Why would you say that?"

"Other kids had parents bringing them to lessons. They'd be there cheering them on during concerts. Hers? Not once. I saw her cry a few times when she thought no one was looking."

Julia used to cry at the symphony? She'd never told him. Never complained. It had bothered him that her parents had all but abandoned her, but she'd seemed okay with it. Learning there had been a time she'd loved him more than her music had been like a dagger to his heart. How was it Owen Baker was the only one who knew this about Julia?

"But you were looking?" Rhys asked, thinking to himself it sounded as if Baker's actions had been more like spying.

"Not like you're trying to imply. She was there a lot." Baker fidgeted in his seat. "What does all this have to do with Diana?"

Joshua paused, waiting for Rhys's nod before proceeding. "We have witnesses who claim you were obsessed with Julia Harcourt. You stalked her. Wrote her fan letters."

Baker's face reddened as he smacked the table. "That's not true. If there is a witness, he or she is lying. If you want to speak with someone obsessed with Julia Harcourt, you should question Lewis Vogel. That guy has had it out for her since they were kids. He hated her, probably because he was in love with her. I wouldn't be surprised if he had asked Julia out and she said no. He didn't take rejection well. Diana told me he'd once asked her out, and when she turned him down, he got real angry at her. Called her all sorts of names."

Interesting that Owen Baker was so quick to cast blame on Vogel. Even more interesting was that Vogel had a connection to Diana.

"Diana looked a lot like Julia, didn't she?" Rhys asked.

"I don't know. They both had blond hair, but since I never stalked Julia, I can't say if they looked alike, because it's been years since I've seen her. I still don't understand why you're asking me about Julia Harcourt. What does she have to do with Diana's murder? Was Julia another one of the Composer's victims?"

Rhys ignored Baker's questions. "Where were you last night?"

Looking away, Baker resumed tapping his fingers

on the table. "Where I've been for the last month. The mountains."

"See, I think you're lying," Rhys said, ready to break apart Baker's so-called alibi. "I think you came back a few times over the past month. I think you knew the sheriff wanted to speak with you, which was why you didn't let anyone know you were back or where you were going."

"Sheriff Pearce didn't care about finding Diana, but I knew if he changed his mind, I'd be his only suspect, and I'd wind up behind bars represented by a court-appointed defense attorney right out of law school. I wouldn't be the first one from the mobile home park to go down for a crime I didn't commit in this town."

Joshua frowned but didn't come to his boss's defense. Unfortunately, there was nothing he could say since Baker was speaking the truth, at least about him being the only suspect in Pearce's mind. The sheriff had made that clear to Rhys at the crime scene. As for innocents being railroaded for crimes, Rhys couldn't speak to that. He didn't live in Laurel Creek anymore. But if it were true, he couldn't imagine Joshua being a part of it, even passively.

"So, you admit you didn't spend the whole month in the mountains," Rhys confirmed. "You came back to town."

"I might have," Baker said slowly. "Just to check on the status of Diana's case and to pick up some provisions."

Rhys pinned Baker with his glare. "Did you happen to be home this morning?"

"I have the right to defend myself and my property."

"I'm taking that statement as an affirmative to my question." Rhys reached up to feel the large bump hiding underneath his hair. "You don't have the right to concuss a federal law officer."

Baker had the good sense to look apologetic. "It was just the handle of a rake. I didn't mean to hit you that hard. I thought you were there to steal my stuff."

"You can use that as your defense in court," Rhys said. "Shame it's your second assault charge. Prosecution might not be willing to let you plead to a lesser offense. But I suppose I could put a good word in for you."

Baker sighed. "What do you want?"

"Handwriting sample."

Baker didn't hesitate. "No problem, man. But I'm telling you this now. I didn't hurt Diana Crain or any other woman. You're barking up the wrong tree."

Rhys pushed back from the table and stood. "We'll see about that, won't we?"

The handwriting sample would be a good start, but there was a lot to unpack from the interrogation.

Joshua followed Rhys into the hall. "What do you think?"

Rhys scratched his nose. "I think he's hiding something, but I'm not sure it has anything to do with the Composer." It was still possible Diana's murder had nothing to do with Rhys's case. This could all be a coincidence. "I'm going to have my people find out where he stayed while he was in the mountains."

"You think he's lying about being there?" Joshua asked.

"I'm not sure. Lying about being there or lying about *why* he was there. Maybe it has nothing to do with Diana's murder or the Composer. It's just a gut feeling."

Joshua nodded, glancing down the hall to where Julia was reading her book. "Tomorrow's Friday."

"Yeah, so?" Rhys had no idea what that had to do with Baker.

"You and Julia need to eat, right? Bring her to Sabbath dinner." Joshua smiled. "Sam's been texting me all week about Julia and you, and asking how things are going."

Rhys chuckled. "It's like he's still fourteen."

"He liked Julia. We all did, even Dad."

He found he liked the idea of Julia having dinner with his family. She'd spent so much time at his house back in high school, she'd practically been one of them. Even though she was technically half Jewish and her parents hadn't raised her in any religion, Julia had loved attending their weekly Sabbath dinners. "I'm not making any promises, but I'll try." Between his case and his complicated relationship with Julia, he wasn't sure now was a great time for rekindling her connection to his family. "Ready for what we discussed?"

"I'm ready." Joshua wrapped his hand around the interrogation room's doorknob. "Let's see how good of an actor Owen Baker can be."

Chapter Eleven

Back aching from sitting in one of the waiting room's plastic chairs, Julia raised her head as Rhys appeared in front of her. "Is it over? Is Owen Baker the Composer?"

Rhys shook his head and grabbed her hand. "Come with me. I wish I could tell you he broke down and confessed, but the truth is, it's rarely as easy to get a confession as they make it seem on television. In a moment, Joshua is going to take him to a holding cell, where he'll wait to be arraigned on hindering a law enforcement officer's duties and assault charges for whacking me on the head."

"Owen gave you the concussion?" She walked with Rhys down the hall toward the interrogation room.

When he had filled her in on his plan, she'd been eager to help. But now, she was petrified. What if Owen Baker was the Composer? Coming face-to-face with the man who'd terrorized her and killed all

those women made her want to run out of the building. She laced her fingers with Rhys's.

"He did," Rhys said. "He confessed to that much."

No matter what happened, Rhys would protect
her. She didn't know what was happening between
them, but if it involved more of what they'd done
earlier, she was all for it.

It was one thing to bonk someone over the head
and another to murder multiple people. "What do
you think? Is he my stalker?"

"I don't know, Julia." He tucked a strand of hair
behind her ear. Rather than wearing it in a neat bun,
she had left it down and loose like she had as a teenager. "I know he's hiding something, but then again,
who isn't? He's giving us a handwriting sample for
comparison. If he did author those letters, the FBI
handwriting analysts will figure it out, but even if
he was your stalker, that doesn't automatically mean
he's the Composer. It's just a theory until there's evidence to support it."

She and Rhys stopped a few feet past the interrogation room. Rhys sent a text to Joshua, and a minute later, Joshua and another man came through the
door. Although it had been years, she recognized
Owen Baker. He hadn't changed much except for
his hair, which he used to wear much shorter. She
held her breath. Since becoming an adult, she'd lost
most of her face's roundness and gained that full-
ness at her bust and hips. The question was, would
he recognize her?

Joshua led a handcuffed Owen in their direction. She held her breath, waiting for Owen's reaction.

But there wasn't one.

The second Owen spotted Rhys and her in the hallway, he angled his head away from them, as if he didn't want to be seen in his current state. To Julia, that seemed like a normal response to being arrested. Owen didn't give her a second look. He didn't appear to recognize her. If he was her stalker, wouldn't he have reacted to her presence?

Owen disappeared around the corner. The holding cells, as well as the county detention, the county's local jail that held nearly two thousand inmates, was located in the building next door, but there was a tunnel connecting the two buildings.

She turned to Rhys. "He didn't recognize me."

Rhys seemed as if he were deep in thought. "Didn't seem to."

They headed out the front of the station to the car. "If he is innocent, I feel bad for him. I mean, he just found out his girlfriend is dead, and now he's in jail, a suspect in her murder."

Giving her a soft smile, Rhys squeezed her hand. "You have a big heart, you know that?"

She knew he meant it as a compliment. In some ways, she'd come to view her empathy as a curse. "I want to believe the best in everyone. It's my biggest flaw, because I'm constantly getting disappointed when people don't act the way I expect them to."

Luckily, as a musician, she had the opportunity

to channel her emotions into her compositions. If she didn't have that outlet, she didn't know where she'd be.

Rhys walked her to the passenger side of the car. "Like your parents." He brushed his knuckles down the side of her neck, eliciting chills. She wasn't even sure he'd done it consciously. "And me. Baker remembered you being sad a lot of the time."

It was strange to talk about this with Rhys after all these years. She'd thought she'd put those days behind her. But the past had a way of sneaking up on her when she least expected it. "I wouldn't say a lot of the time, but sure, there were times I found a quiet corner to cry in. I'm surprised he noticed. I didn't think anyone had seen me."

Rhys twirled a strand of her hair around his finger. "He watched you a little closer than what I'd deem normal. Daniel said that years ago he'd caught Owen going through your backpack during practice."

That kicked up a memory. Most of the stalker's letters had been placed in either her home's mailbox or mixed in with the mail at the symphony. But there had been a couple of exceptions. "I found a letter in my backpack once in the front pocket. I had no idea how or when it got in there."

She'd carried the bag to school and to music practice, but it hadn't always been in her possession. Anyone could have slipped it inside when she hadn't been looking, and since she hadn't used that front pocket for anything, it could have been there for months.

Knowing the stalker had the ability to touch her personal items had creeped her out more than the letters.

Rhys tipped up her chin. "I hate that you felt as if you couldn't tell me you had a stalker or that you cried during violin lessons. I understand why now, but it bothers me to think you kept things from me."

Did he realize he didn't stop touching her? Her hair, her cheek, her chin. It was as if he were publicly claiming her, his actions making it clear to everyone she belonged to him. He used to do it all the time when they'd dated. She wasn't sure what his behavior meant. Had he changed his mind from this morning?

How dare he throw her secrets back in her face. She shoved him away with both hands. "Like you were honest about your feelings for me? We both kept secrets from one another." He wanted to know her secrets? She'd give him one. "The song the Composer is tattooing on his victims? It's called 'Waterfall.' It's about you and me and the innocence of first love."

His expression softened, the tension from his jaw and the hardness in his eyes melting away like ice. What was he thinking? Her heart fluttered, and her pulse skipped as she waited for him to speak.

Rhys grabbed her by the shoulders. "Did you tell anyone else about the meaning behind this song?"

Her stomach sunk. Out of everything he could have said, that was what he wanted to know? She and her big heart never learned. "The whole orchestra knows it's a love song, but they don't know it's ours." She threw her arms up in the air. "That's all you're going to say? I tell you I wrote a song for you, and your re-action is to wonder if it can help you solve your case?"

He rubbed his temples. "What do you expect from me, Julia? It's been a long day and my head is pound-ing."

A twinge of sympathy for him almost made her stand down. On top of his concussion, he'd passed the state of exhaustion hours ago. Then he'd whisked them down to the sheriff's station and interrogated Owen for more than an hour. She had no idea how he was still standing.

But he wasn't the only one who was tired. She was tired of not fighting for what she wanted. And what she wanted…was Rhys.

"I want to know if you're at a place in your life to open yourself up to all the responsibilities that come with being in a relationship." She couldn't believe they were having this conversation in the sheriff's department's parking lot, but it couldn't wait any lon-ger. "You kissed me. Did it mean anything to you?"

"It did. It meant a lot to me." He hung his head and blew out a breath. In an instant, she knew what he was about to say. "But it can't happen again. I care about you. I'll always care about you. But I'm never going to be a relationship guy. I'm married to my job, and that job is based out of Atlanta."

How could he say he wasn't a relationship guy when they'd had a relationship throughout high school? It was just an excuse. The truth was he didn't want a relationship with her. And while she didn't understand it, she could accept it. But his constant back and forth infuriated her.

She waved a finger at him. "You kissed me, remember? After you made it clear this morning that I meant nothing more than a case to you, I lowered my expectations and accepted at most we might find the way to one day be friends. I apologized to you because I'd acted unreasonable. And what do you do? Come home and kiss me. Don't blame me for getting the wrong idea about us. That's on you."

He sighed. "You're right. I'll admit, I get confused around you. You slay me with your beauty and your talent and your big heart. I'm honored and floored that you composed a song about us. If I had it in me, I'd give you everything you want. The house, the 2.5 children, the white picket fence, all of your dreams. But my reaction to your revelation about 'Waterfall' was a telling one. It's not in me to give you what you want, and I can't lie to you and say that will change in the future."

If she'd learned anything in the last few days, it was that each day was a precious gift meant to be savored. All the Composer's victims had probably believed they had years of life ahead of them only to have a serial killer cut it brutally short. They'd been robbed of their futures.

She stepped closer to him. "Let me get this straight. You don't regret kissing me, but you are worried kissing will give me the wrong idea about us?"

He frowned as if he wasn't sure what answer to give. "That's a fair statement."

"You're making decisions for me again, Rhys. Shouldn't I have some say?" she asked.

He swallowed. "Yes?"

"What if I told you I don't need promises of the future? What if I told you I'm good with just seizing the moment?"

"I'd say…" He pulled at his collar. "Can you be more specific?"

She hung her arms around his neck. "Specifically, yes to kisses, no to commitments and expectations. When the danger passes, we both move on, no hard feelings."

It was the perfect plan. They were both attracted to each other, and as long as the situation required for Rhys to stay in her home, they might as well enjoy their time together. It would eliminate his apprehension of giving her the wrong idea and alleviate his guilt that he was taking advantage of her. No matter what happened between them during this time, she was going to hurt when they said goodbye again. But she refused to live with regrets.

He reached behind her and popped the passenger door open. She skirted around him, placed a hand on the top rim of the door and peered over her shoulder at Rhys. "So, what do you say to my offer?" she asked.

His gaze dropped to her lips. "I say—"

About to slide into the car, she spotted a bloody

mass on the passenger seat and froze. She turned away, bile rising in her throat. "What is that?"

He gently pushed her to the side and bent to take a closer look. "It's a heart. It looks human." He looked up at her with concern. "There's a note here too. You know what this means?"

She knew exactly what it meant.

Owen Baker couldn't be the Composer.

And the serial killer had claimed one more victim.

Chapter Twelve

Carrying a six-pack of beer, Rhys got out of his rented vehicle and walked around to open Julia's door. It had been a busy twenty-four hours, and he was grateful to have Friday night off from work. He'd spent all night at the sheriff's station and a majority of the day on-site of the most recent Composer crime scene.

A state park ranger found the body of Alexis Robinson on the Appalachian Trail at five that morning. Her girlfriend had reported her missing to the Laurel Creek Sheriff's Department in the middle of the night after Alexis had failed to come home after work. She'd seen the news and worried the slim blond-haired Alexis had been taken by the Composer. Unfortunately, her fears had been warranted.

The coroner had determined that Alexis's heart had been removed postmortem. Rhys's call to the BAU had provided him with theories for the Composer's change in modus operandi. The removal of the heart was symbolic, possibly representing the killer's heart or the victims', but likely representing Julia's heart since it had been found with the note in the passenger seat of Rhys's car.

The note had been short and to the point, ordering her to leave town to avoid the same fate as the other victims. The handwriting analyst had confirmed it was transcribed by the same author as the previous letters and that the person was not Owen Baker. Unfortunately, that didn't eliminate him as a suspect in Diana's murder. It was possible that there were two killers running around in Laurel Creek or that Julia's stalker wasn't the same person as the Composer. Both ideas seemed ludicrous in Rhys's opinion, but he couldn't take them off the table at this point.

After finding the heart, he and Julia had gone back into the sheriff's office to report it to Joshua. It had been a blessing that Pearce had already left for the night, having completed his press conference an hour earlier. Rhys hadn't been certain his brain could handle dealing with the pompous jerk. He'd never bought into the idea of Julia's stalker, and Rhys wouldn't put it past him to accuse her of putting the heart in the car herself.

But this time, the Composer had been caught on video. Joshua had found footage of the man leaving the heart in Rhys's car within minutes of checking the parking lot's security camera. He'd placed the heart in the car after the sun had set, not long after the last of the press had left. Around six feet tall, wearing black pants, a black sweatshirt and a black baseball cap low on his head, it was impossible to see what he looked like. Someone at the FBI would try to clean up the footage to see if they could get a better picture of the man they were searching for.

Rhys had sent Julia home with Deputy Matt Levy, confident that Matt would keep her safe in Rhys's absence. When Rhys had come home to Julia's late that afternoon to catch some shut-eye in the spare bedroom, Julia had been drinking tea and chatting away with Matt's pregnant wife, Ellie, a teacher at the high school.

It was good for Julia to make friends in Laurel Creek. Other than Rhys and his brothers, she hadn't had any close friends the last time she'd lived there. Now he realized he deserved the blame for that. As a teen, he'd monopolized all her free time, which, due to her busy schedule of school and violin, hadn't been much. He regretted robbing her of that opportunity. When he finally caught the Composer and returned to his home base of Atlanta, Julia would need a friend like Ellie.

Rhys's throat thickened as he pondered leaving Julia. Their lives were on two separate paths, and he didn't see how they could possibly converge. It would kill him to one day return to Laurel Creek and see she'd moved on with someone else. But he stood by his statement that she deserved more than he could give her.

With everything that had happened last night, he hadn't had a chance to respond to her offer of a no-strings affair. In a way, he was relieved. He wasn't sure he'd have the strength to turn her down, and while she might have the capacity to separate the physical from the emotional, he couldn't—not with her.

And yet, here he was with her on his arm, walking up the front porch steps to his father's house. In a way, Sabbath dinner was his first date with Julia in more than a decade.

Julia bit her lip. "Are you sure this is okay?"

"It's more than okay," he said. "Sam and Joshua would rather see you than me any day. Plus, you made chocolate cake for dessert. You know the way to Sam's heart is through his stomach."

Julia stared at the two-person swing on the porch where their initials were carved into the wood. "Good to know some things haven't changed." She gave him a small smile, but there was a sadness behind it.

One significant thing had changed.

Them.

Rhys had hidden his true reaction to her admission that "Waterfall" had been written about them. How could he explain in words how much it meant to him? He couldn't, which was why he hadn't tried. He'd let her think it meant nothing instead of everything.

He returned her smile even though they were both lying. "Nope. Things haven't changed."

His childhood home had also remained the same. With its light green siding and bay windows outlined by ornate white trim, the picturesque Victorian-style house was considered one of the neighborhood's most beautiful homes. It was hard to believe from the outside how much chaos had hidden behind its walls.

Rhys and his brothers all chipped in financially to help out their dad. A landscaping company kept the lawn mowed, the snow shoveled and the garden tended. A maid cleaned twice a week and washed their father's laundry. A maintenance man did the upkeep on the house and fixed what needed fixing. And everything else, such as paying the bills and making sure their father ate every day, was left to Joshua. Their father hadn't held a job in years. Sometimes, Rhys wondered if his father even knew what year it was. He rarely came out of his workshop. Rhys couldn't remember the last time he saw him.

The door swung open before Rhys had the chance to knock, and Sam launched himself at him. His twin didn't believe much in personal space.

Sam threw his arms around Rhys and, although they were an equal height and weight, lifted him a few inches off the ground. "It's a miracle. Rhys finally made a Friday-night dinner."

Joshua sauntered up to the door with a smile. "I'm going to wager a guess that Julia convinced him to come."

Used to Sam's antics, Rhys shook his head. "I should have taken that bet because it was the other way around."

Sam pushed Rhys out of the way and went to hug Julia. "I'm wounded. You didn't want to see us?"

She blushed as she accepted Sam's embrace. "I didn't know if it was appropriate under the circumstances."

When Rhys had suggested it to Julia that afternoon, she'd balked and tried to convince him to go without her in order to have some "quality brother time." He would have preferred a quiet evening at home with her to a loud night with his family, but as he'd told Julia, he wouldn't have put it past Sam to show up at Julia's house to pester them until they gave in to going to dinner.

Joshua and Sam had never said as much because they knew it was a sore spot for Rhys, but he knew they missed her. More than a friend, she'd been like a sister to them. Rhys had never explained to them why he'd broken up with her, which was why it must have been difficult for them when she'd left town and never contacted them again.

A deep voice boomed from behind Joshua, one he hadn't been expecting. "Julia, sweetheart, you are welcome in this house whatever the circumstances."

Face freshly shaven and dressed in a light blue button-down shirt and khakis, Griffin Keller beamed with a smile that Rhys hadn't seen in years.

Rhys didn't know whether to be thrilled or incensed. His father hadn't shared a Sabbath meal with them since they'd been kids. And Rhys couldn't remember the time he'd last witnessed him without his scraggly beard. Apparently, his sons didn't warrant an appearance, but the girl from Rhys's past did. "Dad? You're joining us?"

His dad gave him an incredulous look, as if he couldn't believe Rhys would ask such a stupid question. "Are you kidding? I haven't seen Julia in more than twelve years, and that's twelve years too long." He opened his arms wide. "Welcome home, darling."

Julia glanced at Rhys as if asking for permission. No matter how he felt about his father, if she was comfortable with hugging him, Rhys wouldn't object. At his subtle nod, she stepped between Joshua and Sam, walked into the living room and then went into his father's waiting arms. "Thank you, Mr. Keller."

His father's behavior wasn't making a lot of sense to him, and Rhys felt as if he'd missed something. Joshua and Sam didn't act surprised to see him there. But they were closely watching Rhys for his reaction.

His dad patted her on the back and released her. "You're an adult now. Call me Griffin."

It warmed Rhys's heart to see Julia lit up from all the affection. Rhys and his brothers moved inside the house and shut the door. Underneath the scent of dinner was the unique one he smelled every time he came over. It was the smell of home. He glared at his brothers, silently demanding an explanation for their father's unusual attendance. In response, Sam chuckled and Joshua grinned.

Griffin led Julia to the dining room. "It's been entirely too long since we had a woman light the Sabbath candles. Would you do the honors?"

"I'd be honored." She disappeared around the bend with his dad.

Rhys turned to his brothers. "Do you mind telling me what I missed? When did Dad start remembering he had a family?"

"He's been making more of an effort the last few weeks," Joshua said. "All he needed was a little prodding, and he was happy to come to dinner tonight."

A little prodding? That hadn't gotten his father's attention when Rhys had asked him to come watch one of his high school football games or when his boys had begged him to take a more active role in their lives. Sure, he'd shown up for parent-teacher conferences and made sure they got their yearly physical and their teeth cleaned. He'd come to Sabbath dinners now and then, and it was true he'd adored Julia. But when Julia had disappeared from Laurel Creek, he'd never mentioned her to Rhys or asked where she'd gone. To Griffin Keller, out of sight was out of mind. Except if your name was Alicia Keller.

His dad hadn't been negligent per se. Just absent. He walked through life almost in a daze, stuck in his past rather than focusing on what was right in front of him.

Julia recited the prayer over the candles, and they all sat down to eat. Someone had set the table, draping it in a white cloth and setting it with their mother's best china. Small amounts of red wine had been poured into crystal glasses and in the center was a loaf of bread covered with lace. "I haven't had challah in forever," Julia said, referring to the braided egg bread.

After the blessings over the wine and bread, Griffin passed the platter of meat. "Joshua grilled up some burgers. It's probably not what you're used to as a big star—"

"It's perfect," Julia said, putting two burgers on her plate. She always did love her red meat. "Thank you."

Joshua popped off the top of his beer bottle. "Any word from your guys about the—"

"No talking shop tonight, boys," his father said good-naturedly. "Sabbath is meant for relaxation and contemplation. I think all of us can use a break, don't you?"

He wasn't wrong. The purpose of Sabbath was to rest. That was the reason his mom had begun the tradition in their household in the first place. They hadn't been a religious family, but as sheriff, his dad had worked long hours. Having Friday-night dinner together was a way of forcing him to rest and concentrate on his family. Once Rhys's mom died, his dad rarely sat with them at the table on Fridays. A few of those nights happened to coincide with Julia's attendance, but usually, Joshua brought a plate out to the workshop, where their dad spent most of his hours.

Rhys found it strange to hear words like "relaxation" and "no talking shop" coming from his father's hypocritical mouth.

Because it was something Rhys's mother would've said.

Despite the reservations he'd had about his father, dinner was the most fun he'd had in ages. His brothers and his dad had peppered Julia with all sorts of questions about the people she'd met and the places she'd visited. Her stories were lush with detail and oftentimes quite funny. He couldn't remember when he'd last laughed so hard. There was a twinkle in Julia's eyes and a rosy flush to her cheeks from her wine. Rhys suppressed the urge to toss his arm over her chair and sift his fingers through her hair like he used to.

After dessert, his father put down his coffee mug and gazed at Rhys from across the table. "Rhys, can I speak with you? I don't mean to be rude, Julia, but there are a few things I need to discuss with him in private."

Rhys froze in his chair, flummoxed by his father's request. It was completely out of character for him. What could he possibly have to discuss with Rhys that couldn't be said around the others?

Julia nudged Rhys's shoulder. "Go," she whispered, giving him an encouraging smile.

As much as a part of him wanted to protest, the curious part of him prevailed. He pushed back from the table and stood, prompting his father to do the same.

Sam jumped up from his chair and plopped down

in Rhys's. "We'll keep Julia company, Dad. Don't worry." He wiggled his eyebrows. "I bet Rhys didn't tell her the story about the duck."

Oh no. There was no way he wanted Julia to hear that one. He shook his finger at Sam in warning. "Do not tell her that story. You swore an oath it would never get outside the family."

Sam threw his arm around Julia and smiled. "I'm not breaking my promise, Rhys. Julia *is* family."

His brothers laughed and Julia glowed with happiness. Rhys sighed, hoping Sam was just kidding. Once Julia heard that particular story, she'd never look at him the same.

Rhys and his father left the room and headed out the back door toward the workshop. When his parents had bought the house, they'd converted the detached garage into a space for his father to work. His mom hadn't wanted her sons to stumble onto any crime scene photos or documents. She'd insisted violence was not acceptable inside their home. That included all roughhousing. If the brothers felt the need to beat up on one another, they could take it outside to the yard. *How ironic.* The family had kept their promise. Unfortunately for her, others hadn't agreed.

Joshua had been the one to find her body. They'd walked home from school together, but when they'd gotten a couple blocks away, Joshua had challenged them to a race. Being the oldest and fastest, Joshua had beaten them home. With a maturity Rhys had never witnessed before, Joshua had tried to keep Sam and Rhys out of the house. But they'd refused to listen. Rhys was ashamed to say he hadn't believed him. He'd needed to see her lifeless body himself.

It was the worst decision he'd ever made.

Griffin unlocked the workshop door and flicked on the lights. As Griffin made his way to the chair at his desk, Rhys stayed by the door. The room was no bigger than six hundred square feet. From murder boards to newspaper articles about similar killings across the country, every inch of the walls was plastered with information related to his mother's cold case.

Rhys's stomach burned. It didn't ever get any easier to see, and he didn't know how his father could stand to look at it day in and day out. "When did you remember you have three sons? I asked Sam and Joshua, but they were vague about the when and the why."

His father dragged a second chair to the desk and waved an invitation for Rhys to sit. "Sam confronted me a month ago. He told me you were turning into me. It was as if one minute you were ten, and the next minute I looked up, you were a grown man. I missed everything in my grief, and your mother would skin my hide if she knew."

Rhys stayed where he was. "Sam has one conversation with you, and you suddenly see the light. We tried to get through to you for years, Dad. Why now? What's suddenly changed now that we're adults and don't need you anymore?"

Rhys felt like a little kid when his father pinned him with a glare. "Hearing that my sons were out there putting themselves at risk in their jobs but being too chicken to risk their hearts."

That's what he wanted to discuss? Rhys's heart? What right did his father have to dissect Rhys's life after being absent for so long? He should turn around and walk right out the door. It would serve his father right.

But he couldn't. If his dad was worried enough about Rhys to forgo his usual solitude, Rhys needed to hear him out. It was an opportunity he would've died for when he'd been a kid, and he guessed that little boy was still somewhere inside of him.

He collapsed into the chair beside his father. "It's not like that."

His dad kicked his legs out and folded his arms across his chest. "No? So you've fixed things with Julia, then?"

Rhys gritted his teeth. There was nothing to fix. "That's none of your business."

"I'll take that as a no." The wrinkles in his dad's forehead became more pronounced as he frowned. "You were in love with that girl. I expected you two would be the first to give me grandchildren."

The vision of a pregnant Julia holding a little boy in her arms hit Rhys with such clarity, it could have been a memory. He curled his fingers around the sides of the chair's plastic seat. "We want different things now."

Even if there was a chance for them, Rhys knew better than to take it. His father should understand since he was no different. *Like father, like son.*

His father's gaze slid to the framed photo on the corner of his desk of a young Alicia standing in the yard with the three Keller boys hanging from a tree behind her. "You look at her like she's your reason for breathing. That kind of love only comes around once in a lifetime for us Keller men." He leaned forward and clasped Rhys by the shoulders. "It would be a shame to let your fears keep you from what you really want."

Julia helped Sam clear the table while Joshua went to take a phone call. Dinner had been overwhelming but priceless. She'd missed all of them more than she cared to admit. Sam never ceased to make her laugh, but he wasn't all about jokes and fun. It was clear he was the glue that held the family together. But if Sam was the glue, then Joshua was the carpenter, working with the glue to ensure the bond held firm. Then there was Rhys, the sturdy and dependable frame. Each of them played a vital role in the structure of their family. Without one, it would all fall apart.

At the sink, Sam turned on the water and filled the basin with soap. "You're good for him."

Holding a dry rag, she rested her backside against the kitchen counter. "I don't know about that. I haven't done anything."

"You're here. That's all you needed to do." Sam plunged a plate into the water and scrubbed it with a sponge. "This is the first dinner he's come to in weeks, and the only reason he came at all was because of you. But it's more than that. He's always about work, but when he's with you, he's able to relax."

There were occasions in the last several days when she'd glimpsed the boy from her past, but then he disappeared as if he'd been nothing more than a mirage. By his lack of response to last night's proposition, she assumed his answer was no. He didn't even want a no-strings fling with her. He couldn't have made things clearer.

"Didn't you know?" she said, plucking the clean plate from Sam's hand and drying it. "I *am* work to Rhys. The only reason he's with me is because he's protecting me from the Composer."

"Right. You keep telling yourself that." He chuckled, and she didn't know what he thought was so funny. "Do you honestly think he's staying in your house because of the case?"

"Yes," she said automatically. Why else would he be staying there?

He handed her another dish to dry. "And that it's standard procedure for the case's lead FBI agent to babysit a witness?"

She wouldn't consider it babysitting, but the rest was accurate. "Yes."

"And that there's no one else in the FBI who could do it?"

"Ye—"

"No." He shut off the water, took the plate from

her hand and placed it on the counter. "The answer to all of the questions is no. Rhys is guarding you with his life because you are his life. You always have been. It's like he's been in stasis since you've been gone. Breathing but not living. Smiling but never truly happy. But now that you're back, he's the Rhys he used to be."

"You're wrong. It's still all work for Rhys. He just feels a duty to protect me himself because of our past and because he still cares about me. But he's made it clear there's no future for us."

Sam tugged playfully at the ends of her hair. "I don't know what happened after graduation, but I know he loved you then, and I'd bet anything that he more than cares for you now. My brother loves you. I'm asking you not to give up on him."

Warmth permeated throughout her body. She wanted to believe Sam, but she knew better. The longer she clung to the belief things could work between them, the harder it would be when Rhys returned to his life in Atlanta. Rhys didn't love her. It didn't matter if she didn't give up on him.

Because Rhys had given up on her.

Chapter Thirteen

Home from his father's, Rhys locked the door behind
him and brought their Tupperware of leftovers to their
refrigerator while Julia made them each a cup of hot
tea. He shook his head in silent admonishment. Not
home. He might be staying in her house, but it wasn't
his. The refrigerator wasn't *theirs*. Other than the few
items in his suitcase, there was nothing within the four
walls of this house that belonged to him—including
Julia. Forgetting that fact wouldn't do either of them
any good.

It was natural for the lines to blur, especially with
their history. After her offer of a no-strings affair,
it became even clearer that he'd made a mistake.
He should have never volunteered to stay here with
her. Guarding a witness wasn't his responsibility as
a special agent in the FBI. But the thought of anything happening to her made him act irrationally.
The world would stop turning if Julia died. As long
as it was in his power, he'd break all kinds of rules
to prevent it.

With Julia on another continent, it had been easy to pretend she meant nothing to him. Whenever thoughts of her had crossed his mind, he'd pictured her happy. He'd convinced himself he'd done the right thing for her. Now that he knew how miserable she'd been overseas, he could admit he should have done things differently. Julia had been right. He'd made the decisions for them both, and she'd deserved a say in their relationship. He couldn't change the past, but the outcome would have been the same.

There were some people who couldn't be fixed.

Rhys was one of those people.

Julia set two mugs on the counter and heated a kettle of water on the stove. "It was good seeing your family, especially your dad."

Rhys leaned back against the kitchen counter. "Yeah, I wasn't expecting him to be there."

He wasn't thrilled about his family's little ambush tonight. At least, his brothers could have sent him a text as a warning. Instead, they'd set him up.

Seeing his father acting so normal had thrown Rhys for a curve. How many times had he dreamed of that when he'd been younger? Sure, his dad had occasionally made it to Friday-night dinner with his boys and Julia, but he'd never been so present as he'd been tonight. Rhys felt as if his blood were running hot in his veins. His father was only twenty years too late.

What made Sam go to their dad about Rhys in the first place? It wasn't as if their father had been available for them in the past. If Sam was worried about him, he should have come to him directly and not confronted him at a crime scene or gossiped to their dad. Sam and Joshua weren't any different than Rhys, but they didn't see him complaining to their father about it.

Julia placed a tea bag in each of the mugs. "What did he want to talk about?"

From dinner at his father's house to Julia making them a cup of tea before bed, Rhys realized this whole evening had been a scene in domesticity. "You, actually," he admitted.

Julia peered up at him with curiosity. "Me?"

"He…" Rhys couldn't say it. "…was curious about your case."

She nodded. "Oh. Sure, that makes sense. Did he have any insight?"

Ironic. His father had been researching murders in this country for twenty years. If he were capable of thinking about anything other than Rhys's mom's case, he'd probably make an excellent resource.

"No, not really," Rhys said vaguely. "What did you and my brothers talk about while I was in the workshop?"

Appearing nonchalant, Julia shrugged a shoulder. "Nothing big."

He wasn't sure he believed her. But challenging her about it would lead to a discussion he wasn't sure he wanted to have. They didn't need one more long-winded conversation about feelings.

An uncomfortable silence fell, neither one adding any additional details from their conversations with his family.

The kettle whistled, its noise spurring Julia into action. She lifted the teapot and poured its contents into the mugs.

He couldn't hold it in. He might not want this conversation, but they needed to have it. "I lied. My dad and I didn't discuss the Composer case. He wanted to know if you and I were back together."

She averted her eyes as she shoved a mug in his hands. "And what did you tell him?"

"I told him it was none of his business." And it wasn't. There was nothing his father could've said that Rhys would listen to anyway.

Julia carefully sipped from her mug. "Sam basically asked the same thing."

He'd been right. It had been an ambush, with Griffin taking on Rhys and Sam working his magic on Julia. If Joshua hadn't gotten an emergency call from work, Rhys had no doubt he would've been right there with Sam, sticking his nose into where it didn't belong.

The problem with having brothers who cared about him was they had no boundaries. They'd better watch out, because there'd come a day when it would be their turn, and they'd experience what it was like to have their siblings interfere with their love lives.

"What did you say?" he asked, trying to keep the interest from his voice.

"I told him you're only spending time with me because of the Composer case."

She couldn't hide the pain that lingered in her eyes.

Not very fond of tea but too late to tell her so, he placed his mug on the counter and hoped she wouldn't notice. "About your offer…"

"Yes?"

He took her hand. "As much as I want to, I can't accept. You mean too much to me. I can't use you like that, even if you're good with it. We can say it's just a no-strings affair, but we both know it would be a lie. There are so many strings tying us together that we'll never be unable to untangle them."

"Yet you're unwilling to even try to see if we could get back what we once had. I know your life is in Atlanta and mine is in Laurel Creek, but plenty of people make long-distance relationships work. And Atlanta isn't even that far from here."

He couldn't argue against her logic, but she didn't understand. "I can't. I'm sorry. It's not you. It's me."

She dropped his hand. "How cliché. I get it. You don't want a relationship. You don't have to feed me any lines to make me feel better."

"I'm not feeding you lines." He paused, trying to decide whether to share what had led to his decision to end things between them.

Would it only make things worse if she knew the truth?

She needed to know he wasn't lying to her. If he

was going to have a relationship with anyone, it would be her.

Hand on the back of his neck, he strode into the living room. "The night we broke up, I had a ring with me. I'd been planning on asking you to be my wife."

In the process of bringing the tea to her lips, Julia froze. It felt as if a year went by before she moved again, gently setting her mug on the counter next to his. She wandered out of the kitchen, shock evident in her eyes. "I knew…" She passed by him and went to the table across the room where she'd left her violin. "A ring…" she whispered with her back turned to him. Her fingers drifted aimlessly along the length of the violin case. "What changed between our day at the waterfall and that night? Why didn't you ask me to marry you?"

He fought the urge to go to her, remaining in the center the room. Her pain was nearly tangible to him. "My father. I found him in his workshop crying with their wedding photo in his hand. He didn't know I was there." The memory was so clear, it could have happened that night. The same photo still sat on his desk. "He was apologizing to her for ruining her life. Blaming himself for her death. In all the years, I'd never seen him cry. Not even at her funeral."

She peered over her shoulder. "Did he ever know you saw him?"

"No. I never told him." For a brief second, Rhys had considered mentioning it to his father tonight, but he didn't see the point in rehashing the past. Unlike the conversation he was having with Julia, it wouldn't have solved anything.

Frowning, Julia faced him. "Why not?"

How did a son tell his father he'd witnessed his darkest shame? Rhys wouldn't even know where to begin.

"It wouldn't matter, because seeing him like that had burned itself permanently into my memory. Nothing he could say would have made it any better." The lump Baker had given him suddenly throbbed again. "I'd always resented him for neglecting us and for being singularly focused on solving her murder. We had all lost her, but we still had each other, you know? Why weren't we enough?"

As Julia walked toward him, he took a step back. He didn't want her sympathy. He didn't deserve it.

"In that moment, though, I understood," he said. "And I saw my future. Not the one you and I talked about, but the one we'd have. The violence of my father's job led straight to our doorstep and stole my mother from us. I couldn't do that to you or our children. You were better off leaving Laurel Creek and taking the opportunity in Europe."

Ignoring his silent plea for space, Julia brushed her fingertips over his jaw. "You were scared."

He took a step back, escaping the tenderness of her touch. "I was realistic. And I was right. It's all come full circle. You said it yourself—the Composer got angry when you and I began dating. Your life is in danger because of me."

Strands of blond hair fell into her face as she shook her head. "That's ridiculous and you know it. You are no more to blame for the Composer's actions than I am. We didn't murder those women. The Composer was going to snap one way or another. It's normal for you and I to feel some responsibility, but in truth, we can't absolve one of us without the other. Do you blame me because the Composer killed women who looked like me and tattooed them with my music?"

"No. Of course I don't," he mumbled.

"Do you blame your father for your mother's death?"

"Yes," he said automatically. Although he'd just accused his dad of bringing violence to the doorstep, deep down, Rhys knew it hadn't been his fault. But in Rhys's mind, violence and the Keller men were linked together. Breathing out through his nose, he ran his hand over the top of his head. "No. We don't even know if it had anything to do with him being sheriff."

His mother had been shot twice in the chest one hour before Rhys and his brothers had returned home from school.

There had been no signs of a struggle. No signs of an intruder. No evidence at all. If there had been, their father the sheriff would have found it.

Rhys and his brothers had always seen their father as a superhero. But it didn't take more than a day or two for them all to realize, he was just a man and a flawed one at that. Instead of hugging his sons closer, he'd pushed them away. They'd grieved among themselves and lost their childhood as they figured out how to do their own laundry and buy groceries. Only two years older, Joshua had taken on the task of playing substitute father to them. It was a role he still tried to play. They'd all been scarred by their mother's unsolved murder one way or another.

"Then why blame yourself for the Composer?" Julia stood on her tiptoes and kissed his cheek. She headed toward her bedroom, flipping around before she left the living room. "I don't think you broke us up to protect me. You did it to protect you. You were afraid to lose me like your dad lost your mom."

On that parting note, she left his sight. Was she right? Had he sent her away not for her own good but for his? His breath sawed in and out of his lungs.

He started to go to her, to explain, to argue—he wasn't sure what—only to pause at the sound of her bedroom door closing. When she also engaged the lock, he felt it like a physical blow to the chest. This was what he'd wanted, yet he couldn't stop from feeling as if he'd made a grave mistake.

Rhys had no doubt that Julia had shut him out for more than the night.

She'd shut him out for good.

Chapter Fourteen

Sitting on the couch in Daniel Fenske's office, Rhys ended his call with Joshua. CODIS had found a match for the DNA left behind in the glove Julia had pulled off her attacker.

The Composer had killed his last victim.

They were closing in on him.

Rhys smiled. He was really going to enjoy this next part. He'd put off this interview long enough. He should have done it days ago, but he'd gotten distracted by Diana Crain's murder and everything else that had happened this week. It was time he and Lewis Vogel had a conversation.

He strode down the hallway and went behind the stage. The orchestra was rehearsing a song he didn't recognize, and Julia wasn't seated in her normal chair.

Underneath a spotlight, Julia stood front and center with her violin tucked under her chin, sensually writhing her body as she played an aching melody that reached inside of him and twisted his heart. She was so beautiful, she nearly stole the breath from his lungs. The notes climbed to the highest peak, building in pitch and intensity before rapidly tumbling to the bottom timbre. Was she playing "Waterfall," the song tattooed on the Composer's victims? The song about her and Rhys?

This morning, they'd both acted as if last night's conversation hadn't happened. But as the intensity of the music reminded him of what it had been like to lay with her in his arms at their secret spot, he was nearly compelled to go to her.

He shook it off. There would be time later to tell her how much this song meant to him. To tell her she was right and not to give up on him just yet.

Only right now, he wasn't there for her.

He descended the steps at the side of the stage and headed to where Daniel Fenske was conducting. Rhys didn't want to interrupt Julia's performance, but he had no choice.

"Excuse me, Maestro," Rhys said from below the podium, "but I need to speak with Lewis Vogel. If you can tell him to meet me in the lobby, I'd appreciate it."

Daniel nodded but made no other motion to suggest he'd heard him. Rhys strode up the aisle and out the door. Once there, the music stopped.

A minute later, Lewis came storming out. "You better have a good reason for pulling me out of rehearsal and embarrassing me like this. With one phone call, I can have you fired."

Rhys suppressed a laugh. The Vogels might be

connected, but he highly doubted their money and influence went as far as the FBI.

He had enough evidence to charge Lewis with a felony and arrest him, but he'd dealt with men like Lewis Vogel before. Once their attorneys got involved, everything became more complicated. Rhys would never get a word out of Lewis. Better to let Lewis believe he held all the cards. "I need you to come to the sheriff's department to answer some questions."

Lewis Vogel tilted up his chin. "And if I don't?"

Rhys shrugged. "I'll get a warrant."

Taking a few moments to decide, Lewis pursed his lips and narrowed his eyes. "Fine. I assume I can drive myself?"

"If you don't show at the station in ten minutes—"

"I'll be there." Lewis put up a hand. "I want to get this over with. I'll get my things."

Unfortunately for Lewis, he wouldn't be making it back to rehearsal anytime soon. He could kiss his first chair goodbye.

Rhys tailed Lewis's car over to the sheriff's and brought him inside for questioning. Sheriff Pearce had a meeting with the mayor on the golf course, and since Rhys had technically pulled Lewis in for questioning about the Composer case, Rhys and Joshua had no qualms about keeping the sheriff out of the loop for now.

Owen had been arraigned that morning and had pled not guilty to charges of both assault and hindering law enforcement activity. He currently remained in jail on a hundred-thousand-dollar bond.

After Joshua had coordinated a guard for Julia and brought Lewis a bottled water, Rhys and Joshua settled across the table from him and started recording.

Lewis eyed the tape recorder. "I'm not speaking without my attorney present. I know my rights."

Rhys was thrilled to burst Lewis's bubble. "You're not under arrest or in police custody. You came here voluntarily for questioning. You're free to go at any time. But if you think you need an attorney, we can postpone until a later date." He reclined in his chair. "If you have nothing to hide, an attorney wouldn't be necessary, right? Tell me, do you think you need an attorney right now, Mr. Vogel?"

Lewis looked at him with suspicion. "I can go whenever I want?"

"Anytime," Joshua confirmed.

"Fine." Lewis nodded. "I've done nothing wrong. I don't need an attorney."

So predictable. "I didn't think so," Rhys said. "Tell me where you went two nights ago after rehearsal." Lewis was tall enough to be the man caught on video from the sheriff's parking lot.

Lewis examined his nails as if he was already bored. "Same place I always go after rehearsal. I was home all night."

"You claim you were home every night last week. Anyone to verify that?" Joshua asked.

Lewis sneered. "Not unless you want to ask my cat."

What a jerk. Lewis's arrogance would come back to bite him.

Rhys couldn't wait to see it. "What about two nights before that?"

Lewis shifted in his chair. "I don't remember."

"How about I refresh your memory." Rhys pointed to Lewis's bandage. "According to you when I last asked, you cut your hand when you made yourself dinner."

"Right." Lewis played dumb. "You already knew I was home, so why are you asking?"

Five minutes into the interview and Rhys was already sick of hearing the guy speak. He couldn't wait to toss him into a cell and charge him with the murders of the six women. His parents' millions wouldn't get him out of prison. No amount would.

"As you recall, Julia was attacked outside her home that night," Rhys said. "It was fortunate she managed to pull off her attacker's glove…even scratched his hand."

Lewis blanched. "I don't see how this has anything to do with me."

Joshua flipped open a manila file, snagged a piece of paper, then slid it across to Lewis. "That's funny, because we ran the DNA from the glove through CODIS and got a hit. I don't think you'll be surprised to learn it was your DNA found inside the glove. You know, since you'd been wearing it the night you assaulted Julia in her driveway."

Lewis picked the paper up and perused it before setting it back down. "Just because my DNA was inside the glove doesn't mean I was the one who attacked her. It's a small town. I bet I'd tried it on the last time I shopped for gloves at a camping goods store."

It was a good defense. His attorney could use it later at trial.

"Right." Rhys stood. "Would you mind taking off your bandage? If you did cut it with a knife, it would be easy to do a visual confirmation. There's a big difference between a cut and a scratch. We can clear all this up and you can be on your way."

Lewis dropped his head into his hands, his shoulders caving inward.

They had him. Once Rhys matched Lewis's handwriting to the letters, he'd have enough evidence to charge him as Julia's stalker. From here on out, it was a delicate balance between pushing for the truth and not pushing hard enough that Lewis would lawyer up.

"I wasn't going to hurt her," Lewis said. "I just wanted to scare her off so that she'd leave Laurel Creek."

Rhys resisted punching him in the face. "Why'd you want her gone?"

"Why do you think? She took the concertmaster position from me. I wanted it back."

And now, thanks to Julia, Lewis had it. Julia had filled Rhys in on her decision to relinquish first chair to Lewis to prevent him from having his parents fire Fenske.

If Julia hadn't begged Rhys not to, he would have

pummeled Lewis for slamming her into the wall and physically intimidating her. Lewis Vogel didn't deserve the concertmaster position.

"What about the letters?" Joshua asked Lewis.

Lewis scratched his head. "What letters?"

Rhys had no patience for this. "The letters you wrote to scare her when you were teens."

"I never wrote her a letter, scary or otherwise," Lewis said. "It's not my style. I have no idea what you're talking about."

Was it possible he was telling the truth? From the start, Rhys had been working on the assumption that Julia's attacker in the driveway was her stalker, but what if they were two separate people? Could the Composer be unrelated to the stalking?

With the DNA evidence in front of him, Lewis had admitted to being the attacker. Why would he deny authoring the letters?

One piece at a time, it would all come together like a puzzle. Lewis's confession was the corner piece.

"I understand you asked Julia out years ago and she turned you down," Rhys said, referring to Owen's interview statement where he suggested it was possible.

"Is that supposed to be a question?" Lewis asked sarcastically. When Rhys scowled, Lewis continued. "Yes, I asked her out. We were fourteen. She told me she had a boyfriend. I moved on. She wasn't my type anyway."

Rhys dropped his hands to his lap and clenched them into fists. Owen had been right. Lewis had asked Julia out. And she'd never mentioned it to Rhys. How many other boys had asked her out? He silently cursed. Sixteen plus years later and it still bothered him.

Joshua glanced at Rhys's fists and shot him a grin. Then he directed his attention to Lewis. "What about Diana Crain? Is she your type?"

Lewis paused, cracking the joints in his fingers. "Diana? The girl from the antique store? I heard what happened to her. Didn't you arrest Owen Baker for that? He always was a creep."

"You didn't answer my question," Joshua said.

"I may have asked her out once." Lewis clapped his hands together. "She said no. End of story."

"Her rejection made you mad, didn't it?" Rhys asked.

"No."

Rhys raised an eyebrow. "You didn't yell at her?"

Lewis cracked another knuckle. "No."

"Just like you didn't yell at Daniel Fenske the other day or Julia Harcourt in the hallway?" At Lewis's silence, Rhys continued. Lewis knew there were at least two people already who would testify to his temper, and Rhys wagered there were plenty more. "I'd say you have quite a temper."

"Big deal. Lots of people have tempers. I didn't write any letters, and I didn't kill Diana Crain. Why would I? She was a nothing. Yeah, her folks had some money, but it wasn't as if she was an equal, you know? I thought we could have some fun, so I asked her out, and all of a sudden, she starts shaking like a scared little Chihuahua. That girl had problems. I told her to cut it out, but I didn't yell at her. Is that what she told people?"

Rhys imagined Diana's anxiety attack had been in reaction to Lewis's anger over the rejection and not simply him asking for a date. Most people would be intimidated being questioned by the FBI and a sheriff's captain, but Lewis still saw himself as more. His narcissism would be his downfall. "Why'd you ask Julia out if she wasn't your type?"

Lewis shrugged. "She and I were always in competition. I thought if we dated, I could learn more about her weaknesses. Maybe psych her out to get an edge. That's all. I wasn't interested in her romantically. Especially since she was already more than taken." He grinned like a shark baring his teeth. "She was dating you, right? I know you don't want to believe it, but there was something going on with her and Maestro Fenske."

Rhys huffed out a laugh. "You're still singing that song?"

"I'm telling the truth," Lewis said. "He was always watching her. He *still* watches her. It's like his whole face changes when he thinks people aren't looking. That man is in love with her. I swear it. Once, I saw him with her cardigan. He was sniffing it." He scrunched his face. "Really tacky. I tried to get the symphony board of directors to fire him, but they didn't seem to care. He brought in too much money and it was just my word. Not even Julia backed me up. Which is why it made sense that the feelings were reciprocal."

Why should he believe Lewis? Rhys had never witnessed anything inappropriate between Fenske and Julia, and she adored him like a father. This was just a ploy of Lewis's to take the focus off himself and put it on someone else.

There was a knock on the door. Joshua got up and opened it. Their brother Sam stood in the hallway.

"There's two of you? Are you all brothers?" Lewis asked.

Sam took a step into the room. "Sorry to interrupt, but I have some information that can't wait. I need to speak with Special Agent Keller."

"I'll continue the interview," Joshua murmured.

Rhys walked into the hall and shut the door.

Sam looked as if he were about to burst. "We got the soil report back. You were right. The soil didn't originate at the murder site. It was deposited there."

"And?" Rhys asked, wondering why this information couldn't wait until he'd completed Vogel's interview.

Sam handed him a file. "We've got a match."

Chapter Fifteen

Finished with practice, Julia packed up her things and carefully returned her violin to its case. After disappearing with his violin that morning, Lewis had never come back to rehearsal. She hadn't missed that Rhys had left around the same time, sending Deputy Harrison to temporarily replace him as her bodyguard.

Fresh to the sheriff's department, the deputy was thrilled to have the chance to sit in the auditorium and listen to classical music all day. Apparently, he'd played the trombone in his university's chamber orchestra. She'd spent her entire lunch break listening to his stories about college, and it made her wistful for the missed experience. Maybe one day she'd have the courage to go back to school and get that music degree she'd always wanted.

Except for a few stragglers, everyone had left for the night. The entire violin section was going out to the bar for some bonding time, but Julia wasn't in the mood to socialize. Not to mention, it would be

more than awkward to bring the deputy along with
her. But she didn't want to go home either.

Sleep hadn't come easy last night.

Rhys had bought her a ring. He had been going
to ask her to *marry* him.

She hadn't been able to put that image out of her
mind. The bizarre thing was, she'd had a feeling at
the waterfall. He'd looked at her with such intensity,
such love, she'd been sure he was going to ask her
then and there. When he'd dropped her at home and
told her to dress up for a dinner at Verdi's that night,
Laurel Creek's steak house, she'd never felt such joy.
She'd spent an hour curling her hair and putting on
makeup before slipping on a little black dress and
heels, then practiced saying, "Yes, I'll marry you,"
in front of the mirror. A few hours later, that dress
was in a heap at the back of the closet, and she'd discovered her mascara wasn't waterproof. In the span
of minutes, she'd gone from the highest high to the
lowest low.

They'd never made it to dinner. When Rhys had
shown up at her house, he'd come inside, sat her
down and broken her heart. The love she'd sworn
she saw in his eyes by the waterfall was gone and
replaced with a cool detachment. It had been as if
someone had stolen the soul from the boy she'd loved
between the afternoon and the evening. Until last
night, she'd never known why. Then all the missing
pieces had fallen into place.

Rhys had loved her enough to ask her to marry

him, and he loved her still. Sam had urged her not to give up on Rhys, but sometimes love wasn't enough. Unless Rhys conquered his fear of losing her to violence, he'd never be ready to commit himself to her.

Torn from her musings, she snapped up her head at shouting coming from the back of the auditorium. She quickly identified the source.

What was the sheriff doing at the symphony hall?

She left her personal items by her chair and went to find out. "Sheriff Pearce, can I help you with something?" she asked in an overly sweet tone. "I wasn't aware you were a fan of classical music."

Hands on his hips, the sheriff was none too happy at the moment. Dark pink blotches dotted the deputy's throat. His head hung to his chest like a little boy being punished by his father. Judging by the fury in the sheriff's expression, she gathered Pearce was the father in this scenario.

Sheriff Pearce narrowed his eyes at her as he puffed out his chest. "It was just brought to my attention that my men have been assigned to play your bodyguard over the last few days. I know you're a big star over in Europe, but in my town, you are just another citizen. You don't get to rob the resources of my department to satisfy your overblown ego, young lady. If you want a bodyguard, you can pay for one, but my deputies are not your personal security detail. The sheriff's department serves over two thousand residents in this county. We don't have the time or manpower to provide special treatment for a spoiled, manipulative girl."

How had Sheriff Pearce managed to get reelected every four years? He didn't care about Laurel Creek or the people who lived there. Everything he'd just accused her of was wrong. If anyone had an overblown ego, it was the sheriff. Which was probably why Joshua had kept him in the dark. She held back her anger, knowing in the current situation, he had the power, being the one who carried a gun and the ability to arrest her. "I'm not a girl. I'm a woman. And I wasn't aware you didn't know. Captain Keller—"

"Captain Keller answers to me and will be dealt with," the sheriff said, putting a hand up as if to keep her from talking.

"Please, don't fire him," she begged. "He was only trying to protect me from the Composer."

He moved closer, using his height to intimidate her. "I believe the FBI has jurisdiction, and Captain Keller has his own cases to worry about."

"Of course. I didn't mean to—"

"You never mean to, do you?" the sheriff ground out. Spittle flew from the corner of his lips. "You've been a thorn in my side since you were a kid. First making up the stalker to get some attention and now claiming to be the obsession of the Composer."

Refusing to show fear, she lifted her chin defiantly. "You're wrong about me. I've never lied to you."

"Sheriff," the deputy said, "with all due respect, I don't think you—"

"I don't pay you to think," Pearce shouted. "I pay you to do your job. Now, get out of here and go do it."

Looking torn, the deputy chewed on his lip. "Maybe I should call Captain Keller."

The sheriff harrumphed. "Keller is doing all this because he's out for my job. If you want to remain employed, I suggest you leave Keller to me."

Was Pearce delusional? As far as she knew, Joshua didn't want his job. He was only trying to protect her, even if it wasn't within the sheriff's department's jurisdiction. But Joshua could handle himself. This poor deputy, on the other hand, needed her help. "It's okay. I'll be fine," she reassured him.

The deputy pinned the sheriff with an assessing gaze before turning to her with an apology in his eyes. At her nod, he left.

Although she pretended not to be frightened, the fact was, the sheriff gave her the creeps. For a man who'd been elected to protect and serve his community, he seemed awfully reluctant to do it. "Why don't you like me, Sheriff? I never did anything to you."

He brought his face to hers, blowing his garlicky breath on her. "You tried to play me. I have no patience for that. I have an ex-wife just like you. Always telling stories and feeding me lies. You musicians are all alike."

Really? All this was because he was projecting his disdain for his wife onto other musicians? She'd been practically a child when she'd come to him for help. How dare he judge her on someone else's actions.

"I'm sorry to hear about your ex-wife, but I'm nothing like that. Everything I've reported to the sheriff's office has been true." She folded her arms. "You can't lump every musician in with her. I know you don't believe me, but I really did have a stalker when I lived here, and now that I'm home, he's stalking me again."

His boisterous laugh contradicted his animosity. "Home? You might have bought a house here, but Laurel Creek is not your home, and it never will be."

Chills swept up and down her body. The vitriol in his words reminded her of the ones from the letters. Maybe the reason the sheriff never took her stalker seriously was because *he* was her stalker.

And he'd just sent the deputy assigned to protect her away.

If he was planning on hurting her, she wouldn't make it easy on him. She'd kick and scream with all her might. "You're trying to intimidate me into leaving town for some reason, but it's not going to work. If the Composer's threats haven't scared me away, then a hateful man of a sheriff won't do it either. I don't care what you say. Laurel Creek is and always will be my home. So, do your worst Sheriff Pearce."

Pearce inched forward, his hand going to his side, forcing her to back up the aisle. Her pulse hammered out a staccato beat. He was a big guy and fit to boot, but she could probably outrun him. *Maybe.* What she couldn't outrun was a gun.

"Is there a problem here, Sheriff?" Daniel asked as he approached from the stage.

Julia blew out a shaky breath. He might have just saved her life.

"No." As quick as the flick of a light switch, a mask of pleasantness fell over Pearce's face. "No problem. I was just leaving. Good luck with your opening concert tomorrow night."

Daniel shook Pearce's hand. "Thank you, Sheriff. I hope you'll enjoy your season tickets this year."

Why would a man who hated musicians have season tickets to the symphony?

The sheriff left without saying another word to her. It was almost as if he hadn't just threatened her. She tilted her head. Now that she thought about it, he really hadn't said anything threatening. It was more the way he'd said it and the look in his eye. She could've sworn he was about to harm her before Daniel had shown up.

"Since when does the sheriff have season tickets?" she asked Daniel.

Somewhat distracted, he stared at the doors where the sheriff had just departed. "He's been a season ticket holder for more than twenty years. Although he upgraded his seats this year to front row. The county must have given him quite the raise."

It might not be significant, but she needed to tell Rhys. She went to call him and realized she'd left her phone in her purse on the stage.

Daniel frowned at her. "You're pale. Are you not feeling well?"

She put on a smile for him, not wanting him to worry. "I'm fine. Just a little tired."

"What was Sheriff Pearce doing here? Was there a break in the case?" he asked.

"Not that I know of." Rhys had spoken to Daniel before he'd left. Maybe he knew something. "I'm not sure if it's a coincidence, but Rhys and Lewis have been gone all day."

"It's not a coincidence," Daniel said, a muscle twitching in his cheek. "Rhys brought Lewis down for questioning."

She looked up at Daniel. "What if Lewis is the Composer? This could all be over soon."

He nodded. "Yes, I certainly hope so." Again, he stared off in the direction of the doors. "The sheriff had no right to speak to you like that."

Shock speared through her. "You heard?"

"All of it."

How odd. She hadn't known he'd been in the auditorium during their conversation. Then again, she'd been preoccupied by the sheriff's creepy behavior. "I should call Rhys and tell him the sheriff pulled my guard. He'll want to come get me."

Daniel placed a comforting hand on her shoulder. "I'll bring you home."

Just the other day, she'd been embarrassed by Rhys's order she drive home in the deputy's vehicle. But after the events of the past few days, she understood. He'd wanted her with someone trained to protect her. If something were to happen, Daniel would be little more than helpless. "Oh, no, that's okay. I don't think Rhys would want—"

"Rhys trusts me." He squeezed her shoulder, a tinge of what looked like sadness in his expression. "Don't you?"

She'd offended him. "It's not that. Of course I trust you."

"If you want to wait for Rhys, I'm sure he'll be here soon. Come have a cup of tea with me in my office."

She'd always enjoyed their conversations. What would it hurt to wait an hour? Deputy Harrison would report back to Joshua and Rhys would learn she was unprotected here. If Rhys didn't arrive in sixty minutes, she'd call him. "Tea would be nice."

She accompanied Daniel to his office and sat on the couch as he prepared their tea in the kitchenette. They made small talk, discussing things like ticket sales and the weather.

"How are you feeling about tomorrow?" he asked, handing her the paper cup of tea, then sitting beside her.

"Nervous. I always am before opening night. But I'm excited too. How about you?" she asked. "Do you get opening night jitters?"

"Never had them." He smiled. "I have full confidence in my musicians."

Except the orchestra hadn't been at full capacity that afternoon, and it had been obvious, at least to her ears. "What do we do if Lewis is, um…incapacitated?"

"Obviously, you'll retake first chair. You should

have never relinquished it in the first place." As if he were having a seizure, Daniel's entire body shook, spilling the tea and the cup onto the floor. He didn't seem to notice, making no move to clean it up. "Vogel never deserved it, but especially after you returned." Clenching his fists, he rose from the couch, his shoes coming down on the cup and crumpling it.

Something was wrong with him. "Are you okay, Daniel?"

Daniel seemed far away as he answered. "I thought I heard something. It's probably the sheriff snooping around. He was awfully determined to rile you up, wasn't he? Has Rhys considered…no, the idea is too preposterous." He shook his head. "I'll go check it out. Stay here and finish your tea."

The idea wasn't too preposterous. Daniel had come to the same conclusion as she had about the sheriff. "Please be careful."

There was an innocence in his eyes that reminded her of a little boy. "Always."

Minutes passed, and there was no sign of Daniel. Worried for his safety, Julia couldn't drink her tea. Her adrenaline was surging through her system, making her feel as if she'd drunk a dozen shots of espresso. For a woman who spent hours seated with a violin under her chin, she couldn't sit still for a second. Her knee bounced up and down, and her fingers tapped a melody on her thigh. Finally, she hopped off the couch and went to the door, peeking out into the empty hallway.

It was completely quiet.

Where had Daniel gone?

She hesitated at the threshold, tempted to go check on him, but was nervous she'd walk into something she couldn't handle. She chastised herself for allowing the sheriff to send Deputy Harrison away. Rhys wouldn't want her without a guard. Daniel might be tall, but he was as gentle as a butterfly. What if the person who'd made the noise had hurt Daniel? He could be lying there bleeding and waiting for help. What should she do?

She didn't have her cell and hadn't yet memorized Rhys's number, but Daniel had a landline on his desk. She could call 911. Better to overreact and be wrong than to underreact and be dead. She just hoped the sheriff didn't intercept the call.

Julia scrambled across the room. Reaching for the phone, she knocked a file off his desk. A dozen pages scattered to the carpet. She lifted the receiver to her ear when one of the papers caught her eye. Kneeling with the phone in her hand, she snatched the paper with her other. Acid climbed her throat, nearly choking her as she read the contents.

That handwriting.

Those *words*.

This letter was the work of the Composer. The serial killer didn't just hate her. He blamed *her* for making him murder all those women.

Why did Daniel have this?

He'd given Rhys a letter he'd kept from years ago, but this letter referred to recent events. Had someone mailed this letter here and Daniel had chosen to hide it from her? Or was there another explanation for its presence on his desk?

Her gaze fell to the other pages on the floor.

Photos from her performances, articles about her from the internet, clippings from the *Laurel Creek News* about the Composer.

She gagged, dropped the phone and dry heaved over the trash can. Why did Daniel have all of this?

Deep down, she knew the answer to that question.

Only, she was afraid to accept the truth.

Maybe she was wrong. Maybe he had the perfect explanation.

But she wasn't sticking around to find out.

Holding on to the corner of the desk for support, she climbed to her feet.

Arms captured her in their grasp, pressing against her chest so hard, she could hardly breathe. Screaming for help, she fought back as hard as she could, wiggling her body and stomping her feet like she'd done on her driveway. Only this time, the arms held firm.

She couldn't let him take her. If he did, she'd never survive. Just like the others, they'd find her dead body somewhere on the Appalachian Trail naked and tattooed with her music on her back. Fighting was her only chance.

Fingers covered her mouth. She took the opportunity and bit down hard. The Composer growled his displeasure as a piercing pain pinched her neck.

Within seconds, the room blurred. Her eyes grew heavy, and her neck couldn't support the weight of her head. She felt as if she were floating in warm water. What had he injected her with?

A hood descended over her head and tightened around her neck.

Her final thought was of Rhys.

Chapter Sixteen

Rhys held the soil test report in his hand, trying to make sense of it. Pedology, the study of soil, wasn't his thing. He wasn't sure what he was supposed to be looking for.

Sam pointed to a line on the report. "The soil was mixed with mulch."

It was a good thing Sam did understand pedology, because what he pointed out to Rhys didn't include the word *mulch*. But Rhys did understand its implication. "Meaning it was from a garden, right?"

"Exactly. I tracked down the producer of the mulch." Sam gave Rhys a grin that said Rhys was going to be thrilled with whatever was about to come out of his mouth. "With a little persuasion, she happily shared her customer list, and there were three names that jumped out at me." He snatched the soil report from the file, revealing a copy of that list of names. "Owen Baker was the first."

Rhys looked up from the file. "I took a sample for comparison the other day. He's still a suspect,

but he's not Julia's stalker since we had him in custody when the heart and letter were put in my car."

Rhys still couldn't rule him out. Now that he knew
the attack on Julia was unrelated to the Composer,
he needed to reframe the week's events in his mind.
Since serial killers rarely worked in tandem, he hadn't
considered the possibility. Could Baker and Lewis be
working together? They were both quick to blame
the other before shifting their focus to Daniel Fenske.
They could have coordinated it in case they were ever
brought in for questioning and used the heart to throw
Rhys off Baker's scent since he'd been with Rhys when
it happened.

"Yeah, Joshua told me there was another murder,"
Sam said sympathetically. "I'm sorry."

Rhys nodded once. "Thanks. Who are the other
matches?"

"I almost didn't mention it, but Sherriff Pearce is
on the list. And so is Daniel Fenske."

A sense of foreboding suffused Rhys. Could the
sheriff be the Composer? His thoughts went to Diana
Crain. If she had been anxious to walk home by herself, who else would she have trusted to get her home
safely more than Laurel Creek's sheriff? Pearce was
definitely a possibility, but what was his motive?

Rhys hadn't suspected Daniel because he'd had
an alibi for the night Julia had been attacked in her
driveway. Now that Rhys knew that the attack hadn't
been perpetrated by the Composer, he had to look at
Daniel through fresh eyes. There was nothing in his

past to suggest he'd done anything violent, and he'd shown no animosity toward Julia even once. On the contrary, he'd treated her with more affection than her own parents.

At the same time, Daniel was the first person to know about Julia's return and that she was working on an original composition. And both Lewis and Owen had mentioned Daniel's odd behavior when it came to Julia. Rhys had believed Lewis had been making it up because he was jealous, but what if he'd been telling the truth, at least in part?

Rhys needed to get back to Lewis's interview to find out. "I've gotta go. Thanks for your help with the case, Sam." Wrapping his hand on the doorknob, he looked over his shoulder at his brother. "Oh, and next time, stay out of my love life." With a plan in mind, he strode into the interrogation room. "I think we have everything we need at this point, Mr. Vogel."

Joshua raised an eyebrow at Rhys's statement but didn't say a word. Lewis smirked as he pushed back from the table and stood. Before Lewis got to the door, Rhys asked, "Where do you think you're going?"

The smirk melted from Vogel's face. "I'm leaving. You just said we were done."

"No, what I said was we have everything we need." Rhys pulled out his handcuffs but didn't make a move to place them on Vogel's wrists. Because it was a state crime, he didn't have the jurisdiction. But Lewis didn't know that. "Lewis Vogel, you're under arrest for the battery of Julia Harcourt." He turned to Joshua. "Captain Keller, would you like to read Mr. Vogel his rights?"

Panic filled Lewis's expression. "What? You said I could leave at any time and that I didn't need a lawyer."

Joshua got up from the table. "That was before you admitted to assaulting Julia Harcourt."

"Nothing happened," Lewis argued, his gaze shifting wildly between Rhys and Joshua. "I didn't even hurt her. If anyone was injured, it was me." Lewis offered up his bandaged hand as proof.

Rhys nodded in feigned sympathy. "Then you can take her to civil court and sue her for defending herself against a masked attacker. That should go over well with the judge." He smiled. "And your parents."

That was all it took to break him down. Lewis's eyes widened with fear. "What can I do to get out of it? Community service? I know. How about some information on Daniel Fenske that very few people know?"

Rhys should have known a guy like Lewis would have the dirt on his conductor. He wouldn't be surprised if Lewis had used more than his parents' financial contributions as blackmail for the concertmaster position. "If it helps solve the Composer case, then I'm sure the prosecutor will be amenable to making a deal."

"What do you know about Daniel Fenske?" Joshua asked.

Lewis didn't hesitate. "Daniel Fenske isn't the maestro's real name. He changed it when he was eighteen. And he didn't grow up in New York, like he claims. He was raised in a cabin up in the mountains in Laurel Creek County. His real name is Martin Daniels."

Now Rhys was the one who was panicked. Rhys had done a cursory check on Daniel after confirming his alibi with his assistant, Penelope, a few days ago. Nothing about a name change had appeared in his record. Daniel must have paid a lot of money to cover up his past.

"So, the guy changed his name and fudged his background to sound fancier on his résumé. Why do you think that has anything to do with the Composer case?" Rhys asked.

"Martin Daniels's father used to own a tattoo shop in town before they changed the zoning laws and ran him out."

"How do you know all this?" he asked Lewis.

He shrugged. "My parents have a file on him. My parents have files on everyone."

A sickening thought washed over Rhys. *Julia.* "Joshua—"

"On it," his brother said, rushing out the door.

Rhys pulled out his cell phone and pressed Send. Thank goodness he'd put a guard on Julia.

She trusted her mentor implicitly. If Daniel *was* the Composer, that deputy might be the one thing preventing Daniel from making Julia his next victim.

WOOZY, JULIA BLINKED, her head pounding viciously. Her mouth felt as if it were stuffed with cotton balls and her nose filled with the stench of bleach. She couldn't remember anything. Where was she?

Lying facedown on some kind of table, she tried to get up, but her limbs refused to move. Was she paralyzed? She concentrated on her hands and feet. Could she feel them? She wiggled her fingers and toes. Relieved, she blew out a breath. Okay, she wasn't paralyzed but she couldn't move. What did that mean?

She lifted her head a few inches off the table. No, it wasn't a table.

It was a padded chair.

In a blinding flash, her memory came back to her. She'd been in Daniel's office when she'd found one of her letters. Then someone had snuck up behind her, jammed her with something sharp and yanked a bag over her head.

Didn't Rhys tell her that the Composer had injected his victims with an anesthetic to keep them compliant?

That's when she knew she wasn't paralyzed. She was *drugged*. Struggling again to get up from the table, she realized the drugs weren't the only thing keeping her immobile.

She was also *restrained*.

Where had the Composer taken her? Dust motes floated in the air as Julia scanned the room for details. The dim overhead lights buzzed and flickered, giving the room a bluish tinge that almost felt unreal to her. If someone told her she were trapped in a nightmare, she'd probably believe them. She didn't recognize the room, that was for sure. Wherever she was, she was no longer at the symphony.

White paint was peeling and flaking off the walls as if no one had bothered painting in years, and the green shag rug in the corner had definitely seen better days. On the right side of the room was an accordion closet door with horizontal slats. A few feet from her was a cart with some black coiled machine on it. She'd never stepped foot in a tattoo parlor, but it didn't take a genius to recognize it was a tattoo machine. A quick glance behind her confirmed that her wrists and ankles were restrained by leather straps on a reclining tattoo chair.

Was she inside a tattoo shop?

Below the smell of bleach and strong cleaning products was the scent of something rotten, like a dead animal decaying. Her stomach lurched as she thought of the women who had died before her in this room. Was this the smell of murder?

Of course, she didn't want to die, but even worse would be to die on Rhys's watch. It would actualize all his fears. He'd never forgive himself if she perished at the Composer's hand. He'd blame himself for bringing the violence to her door, just as Griffin blamed himself for the murder of his wife, Alicia. She feared he'd succumb to a darkness from which he'd never escape. And she'd hate that for him. Even if it wasn't with her, she wanted him to find happiness and live life to its fullest.

Somehow, she had to figure a way out of this.

A door slammed from somewhere else in the building, rattling the walls. As the sound of footsteps grew louder, Julia's terror increased. Jerking her wrists against the restraints, she prayed that the footsteps belonged to Rhys or another person who'd come to rescue her. But deep down, she knew, the Composer was coming to make good on his threats.

She stilled at the creaking behind her. Someone was there. She heard his panting. Sensed his eyes on her.

There was a rustling noise as his shoes clomped on the room's concrete floor.

Whose face would she see when she cranked her head in his direction?

A part of her didn't want to know.

A part of her already *did*.

Counting to three in her mind, she came face-to-face with the Composer.

And screamed.

Chapter Seventeen

Pacing the floor of Joshua's office, Rhys glanced at the clock. Julia should be done with rehearsal by now. Why wasn't she answering? The only thing keeping him from losing it was knowing there was a deputy sheriff guarding her. It had been the right call to provide her with twenty-four-hour security. Even so, there was a burning in his gut warning him that something was very wrong. Until she confirmed she was okay, that feeling wasn't going to go away. He needed Julia to pick up her darn phone. When he went to voice mail, *again*, he cursed and stormed out of the office.

Down the hall, Joshua was reaming out a deputy. "What are you doing here? Why didn't you answer the phone when I called and why aren't you with Julia Harcourt?"

What was he talking about? Terror coursed through Rhys. He raced over and grabbed the deputy by his shoulders. "Where is she? Is she all right? Why aren't you with her right now?"

The man visibly gulped. "Sheriff Pearce ordered me off security detail. I didn't have a choice. I thought Sheriff Pearce would have told you which is why I didn't call."

"And why didn't you answer the phone when I called?" Joshua asked.

"I didn't want to get in the middle of the fight between you and Sheriff Pearce," the deputy said.

With a loud curse, Rhys released the deputy. He spun around and punched the wall. The sheriff had crossed a line. And Julia was going to pay the price. "That means Julia's alone with Fenske."

Sheriff Pearce chose that moment to come out of his office. "This is the sheriff's department, not a hair salon," he chastised. "Keep the noise down. I'm trying to work."

Rhys had to count to five in his head before he could respond. Otherwise, he didn't trust himself to not slam his fist into the sheriff's smug face. "If anything happens to her, I'm coming after you with everything I have." If he couldn't use his fists, he'd hit Pearce where it would really hurt. "I'll make sure come next election, you're out of a job. And I won't stop there."

Joshua put his hands in front of Rhys, likely to defuse a potentially volatile situation between his brother and his boss. "Rhys, the sheriff—"

"I was only doing the job that this town hired me to do," the sheriff said without apology. "You don't get to waltz into town and take over as if the people elected you to be sheriff." Pearce pivoted to go back into his office. "Anyway, Ms. Harcourt was fine when I left her with the symphony's conductor."

Rhys took a giant step toward Pearce, making sure the sheriff didn't miss out on Rhys's next few words. "Daniel Fenske is the Composer. Because of your ego, you single-handedly gave him exactly what he's been waiting for. An opportunity."

Pearce stopped in his tracks, the blood draining from his face. "I didn't know." He turned to face Rhys head-on. "Fenske is the Composer? Are you sure?"

"We're sure," Rhys said.

"How can I help?" the sheriff asked. It wasn't an apology, but then again, Rhys didn't expect a man like Sheriff Pearce would give one. An offer of assistance was as close to an apology as Rhys was going to get. Rhys would've told Pearce to shove his offer if he hadn't needed the sheriff's connections to certain families in the community.

"The Vogels have a file on Fenske. I need it. *All* of it," Rhys told Pearce. At the moment, he didn't have time to waste thinking of all the reasons the Vogels kept files on the people of their town. For now, he was simply thankful they had it.

"I'll get it for you," Pearce said. "They owe me a favor."

Rhys didn't doubt that. In fact, he'd been counting on it. The sheriff gave Rhys a curt nod before striding down the hall toward the back exit of the building.

Joshua and Rhys headed in the opposite direction. The Laurel Creek Symphony was only a couple minutes away by car. At the ringing of his cell phone, Rhys hit Accept and put it up to his ear. "Sam? Now's not a good—"

"I'm at the symphony. Julia's not here—no one is—but her purse, her violin, everything of hers is still on the stage. You need to come here, Rhys. I think the Composer kidnapped her."

HER WORST FEARS REALIZED, a tear slipped down Julia's cheek. "Daniel."

He stalked around the tattoo chair, his fingertips caressing her arms. She shivered with revulsion. In all the years of knowing each other, they'd barely even hugged, and now he was touching her as if she belonged to him.

When he stopped in front of her, she raised her chin.

It was the man she knew…but not.

The first thing she noticed was his hair. She wasn't sure why it mattered, but it stood out. His normally immaculate hair was untidy, his side part gone. She couldn't remember a time Daniel wasn't the picture of perfection. The other difference was in his eyes. His enlarged pupils ate up the irises, making his eyes appear black and blank of emotion. Was Daniel still in there?

Clutched in one of his hands was a black garbage bag.

She couldn't tear her gaze away from it.

Would he suffocate or tattoo her first? She'd never asked Rhys for the details of the victims' murders. He probably wouldn't have told her anyway. She'd been so angry at him for keeping things from her, but now she understood he'd only been trying to protect her. It was better not to know.

If she was going to make it out of this, she needed to appeal to Daniel's humanity—assuming he had any. Julia had an advantage that the other Composer victims did not: she and Daniel shared a long history. Maybe it was her big heart talking, but no matter what he'd done to the others, she couldn't believe he'd do it to her.

"Daniel, you don't have to do this," she said, trying to reason with him. "You can let me go right now. I'll tell Rhys that you weren't yourself when you… hurt those other women. I know you didn't mean it."

The man she'd thought of as a father figure picked up a butcher knife and calmly sat down in the wheeled chair beside her, placing the garbage bag on top of the cart. "I remember the first time I met you. It was in Paris. Your parents invited a handful of their acquaintances to their hotel suite to show you off. You wore some ridiculous pink frilly dress with your hair all done in ringlets and patent leather shoes on your feet. But your eyes…it was as if I recognized something in them. I saw into your soul that day. You were miserable. Lonely. Desperate for your parents' love. Until you picked up your violin and began playing.

Then you became transformed. You glowed with radiance like an angel from heaven. You reminded me so much of my mother. I think I told you, you look just like her."

"You did," she whispered, her throat so dry that she was barely able to get the words out. If she reminded him of his mother, why did he want her dead? And what was he going to do with that knife?

Her parents had never told her Daniel had first heard her play in Paris. It hadn't been the first time they'd invited strangers into their hotel suite to hear her play the violin. His would have been just another nameless face in a crowd to her. She didn't recall meeting him before moving to Georgia.

"So, I convinced them to let me be your teacher for your high school years," Daniel said. His voice had taken on a dreamy quality to it. "They were so eager to turn you into their image of perfection, so eager to dump the responsibility of raising you, they didn't even do a background check. All they cared about was that I was a musical prodigy and promised to make you a star. Your parents had carefully chosen their attendees that day. Every one of them was invited for the sole purpose of taking you off their hands. I couldn't let anyone else have you. That talent had to be cultivated. Nurtured. I did that for you."

His story didn't ring true. Although they'd barely spent time with her, they had wanted her to stay with them on tour. Julia had been the one to beg her parents to let her return to the States for the opportunity of having a normal teenage life. If they had sought out a violin teacher for her, it had been done for the purpose of fulfilling her request. Somehow, his depraved mind had rewritten the past to make him out to be the hero. But she wasn't about to argue with him about it. "You did nurture my talent. And you took care of me. Which is why I don't understand why you want to hurt me."

Rolling closer, he snapped on a pair of latex gloves and raised the knife in the air. "I don't want to hurt you. I want to save you."

Her heart was pounding so hard, she felt as if it would explode in her chest. She squeezed her eyelids shut, waiting for the blade to plunge into her spine. "By suffocating me and tattooing me with my music?"

"By setting you free," Daniel said. The knife slit its way down the back of her blouse, baring her skin to the air. "I should have fought back. It was my fault he killed you."

Julia dug her fingernails into the skin of her palms. Even with the rest of her clothes on, she felt exposed. Binding her prostrate to a chair, injecting her with an anesthetic and cutting her out of her shirt with a knife were acts of intimidation meant to show his power over her and make her feel vulnerable. "Fought who? Rhys? He's not to blame for this. You are."

"Not Rhys. Daddy." He bent his head to whisper in her ear. "I'm sorry, Mama. I didn't know what to do. I was scared."

He thought she was his mother?

She rotated her neck to the side to look at him.

He'd mentioned more than once that she reminded him of his mother. Now she understood. Somehow in his mind, he'd gotten the two of them tangled up together. Would it help to break him out of his delusions, or would it only make things worse?

Her body was trembling uncontrollably, her stomach was still queasy and her thoughts were muddled from the drugs in her system, but one thing was clear. She needed to keep Daniel talking as long as possible to buy Rhys enough time to find her, even if that meant playing along with his delusions. "You were afraid. What could you have done?"

"I did it," Daniel said so quietly that she almost couldn't hear him. "I let him punish you, but I'm the one who stole his funny medicine."

"Funny medicine?"

"The brown powder Daddy keeps in his drawer by the machine." *Heroin.* Daniel spoke in the voice of a child, whispering close to her ear. "I took it so he wouldn't hurt you anymore. He got mad and I hid in that closet." His gaze jumped to the corner closet she'd noticed earlier. Then he jolted upward in his seat, raising the knife in the air. "He jabbed you with a needle," he shouted, "and put you on the chair facedown. Then he put the plastic over your head. When he left, I took it off your head, but it was too late. You wouldn't wake up."

Julia swallowed down the fear and revulsion of watching Daniel deteriorate before her eyes. He'd been reenacting his mother's murder over and over again. How had he so successfully hidden his insanity for all these years? Were there signs she'd missed? Had his descent into madness been a gradual progression, or had it turned on like a light switch one day?

"What happened next?" she asked.

His head dropped to his chest. "Daddy stuffed you in a bag and took me for a hike in the woods. Then he dumped you out like you were trash and kicked you over the side of the mountain. No one ever found you. You were just gone."

Bile climbed her throat. A very small part of her pitied him. He'd watched his father murder his mother. She couldn't imagine what that would have been like. As much as she wanted to, she couldn't just stop caring for Daniel. He'd gone through something truly tragic. But that didn't give him a free pass to murder. "What about your father?"

Daniel hurdled out of his chair. "You were lucky to have parents who ignored you. Daddy made sure I learned my lesson every day. I found the chest of instruments Mommy had hidden for us in the woods. He would have thrown them over the mountain just like he'd done to Mommy if he ever found them. Do you know, my mother taught me how to play violin when I was three years old, and that by four years old, I could not only read music, but I could also play almost any instrument? I wouldn't let him take my music from me."

A part of her was sad for Daniel. He'd been a victim of his circumstances. Who might he have been if he'd been raised in a different environment with someone who had nurtured his talent?

The tone of his voice led her to believe Daniel had survived years of torture at his father's hand. He spoke as if he'd returned to the present. Which meant Julia was herself again and not his mother. But how long would it last?

One thing didn't make sense to her. "Why do you tattoo your vict—the women?"

"They shouldn't be forgotten." He stood over her now, his gloved fingers tracing a pattern on her back. "I leave them where they can be found. Mama should have been found."

"That machine you mentioned near the brown powder. It's a tattoo gun, isn't it?" she asked. *Had the one on the cart belonged to his father?* "You want more than for the women to be found. You want everyone to know who was responsible for your mom's death."

He crouched down beside her chair. "Do you forgive me, Mama? It's all my fault. He killed you because of me."

She cried for them both. For the little boy who blamed himself for his mother's death and for herself, who feared she'd never get out of there alive. "There's nothing to forgive. You were only a child. But you're hurting me now. You need to let me go," she begged.

He kissed her cheek. "I can't do that, Julia. I've

been dreaming about this moment for fifteen years. Once I do it, I can stop." He smiled as he lifted the tattoo gun. "It ends with you."

Chapter Eighteen

Rhys held one of the Composer's letters in his hand. Something had happened in Daniel's office. There were two cups of tea: a barely drunk cold one resting on the desk and a crushed one on the floor in front of the couch. Papers were scattered along the carpet. The page in Rhys's hand was written recently. He put it down on the desk and rifled through a stack of papers for a sample of Daniel's handwriting. It didn't take long for Rhys to find some notes Daniel had apparently taken during rehearsal. He compared the notes to the Composer's letter.

It was a perfect match.

"Deputy Levy checked Fenske's house," Joshua said, getting off his phone. "It was all clear. They're not there."

As hope withered, Rhys broke out in a cold sweat. "Anything to suggest where he took her?"

He felt as if he'd just woken up from one of his recurring nightmares in which he and Julia were swimming in the lake when she was yanked under the water. When he tried to get to her, he found himself ensnared by thick vines that wound around his legs and held him immobile. He fought against the tangles, kicking and slashing at them with the knife that had suddenly appeared in his hand. She was right there, right in front of him, but he was completely helpless to do anything. Even though she was beneath the surface, he heard her screams. It wasn't until he gave up his struggle that the vines finally released him. By the time he found her, it was too late.

She was already dead.

Rhys's cell buzzed with a call from the sheriff. He put his phone on speaker. "What do you have for me, Sheriff?"

"Daniel Fenske, born Martin Daniels, attended Laurel Creek Elementary, then fell off the radar in fourth grade, as did his mother," Sheriff Pearce said. "Father was a tattoo artist who worked illegally out of his home after the town forced him to close his shop. Numerous domestic calls prior to the mother's disappearance. She was assumed to have abandoned her family. Father died eighteen years ago from a drug overdose." Rhys heard the sound of pages turning. "Here's something. Fenske's mother was a musician. And get this. She played the violin."

Just like Julia.

Was that Daniel's motive? He killed women because he hated his mother for abandoning him to his abusive father? As far as he knew, none of the other women played the violin. He chewed on his thumbnail. Daniel's motive was irrelevant at this point.

When Rhys apprehended him, the BAU could have a field day figuring it out. Right now, the only thing that mattered was locating Julia.

"We'll find her," Sam said, giving voice to Rhys's thoughts and placing a hand on his shoulder. "Don't give up or blame yourself. Don't be like Dad."

Don't be like Dad. Until now, he'd thought the nightmare about Julia drowning had meant there was nothing he could do to prevent her from dying and that being with him would inevitably lead her to her death. Now he realized he had missed a vital part of the dream. *The struggle.* The vines weren't an outside force keeping him inert. The vines were Rhys. He was struggling against himself. The sooner he learned to let go, the sooner he'd be able to get to Julia. He couldn't waste what little time he had blaming himself for her predicament.

He loved Julia.

He *would* save her.

"I'm not giving up," Rhys said. "I know where he took her. Sheriff, I need the address of Fenske's childhood home."

It explained why Daniel knew the trails so well. He'd grown up in the Blue Ridge Mountains. Daniel wasn't parking his car at one of the public lots and hiking in. He drove his victims to his father's house in the woods, tattooed and killed them, and carried them from his house. If there wasn't an address on file, they could narrow down the search area, but he was praying the Vogels had been sufficiently thorough in their invasion of Fenske's privacy.

As Pearce listed off the address, Rhys pulled it up on his phone's map. It wasn't far, but the roads were tricky in that area. Narrow, rocky and winding, they weren't much more than hiking trails with auto access. And if he got stuck behind another car, there was no bypass. Rhys had never been more at nature's will than right now.

But he didn't care if he had to run his way up the mountain.

He would get to Julia before it was too late.

THE MONOTONOUS BUZZ of the tattoo machine had become one with the buzzing of the lights. It was as though there was a swarm of bees flying all around her. The noise filled her ears, drowning out everything else. Her lips were dry, but she couldn't make the motion to lick them. And even if she could, she didn't think she had any saliva left in her mouth. Her head pounded from a vicious migraine, making every noise, every light, every touch excruciating. But Julia couldn't do anything but lie there on the table and take it. She had lost track of how much time had passed since Daniel had begun the process of tattooing the notes of "Waterfall" onto her back.

Daniel had given her another shot of something that made it impossible for her to move her limbs, but it hadn't been enough to knock her unconscious or even numb her. Although he hadn't said so, she had a feeling that was the point. She knew that people got addicted to tattooing their bodies and found the pain enjoyable, but she obviously had a low threshold for it, because to her, every single jab of the needle in her back felt as if he were injecting fire under her skin.

To escape the never-ending stabbing pain of the needle punching into her skin, Julia retreated into some of her fondest memories of her and Rhys. Kissing on top of the Ferris wheel at the county fair while his brothers heckled them from below. Baking a cake together for Joshua's birthday only to eat it themselves before they had the chance to surprise him with it. Looking up at a sky full of stars and making a wish on a shooting one. Their legs intertwined as they held each other in the water by their waterfall. Each and every memory played on the screen of her mind in high definition. She pretended she could hear his brothers' laughter, smell the chocolate of the cake, see the brilliant stars, feel his body against hers.

Getting lost in her memories of Rhys was the only way she would survive this torture.

RHYS STARED AT the horror in front of him. Daniel had Julia splayed out facedown on an old, cracked leather chair. From first glance, it appeared as if he had sliced open her blouse. Rhys could hardly think of the blade of a knife coming that close to her spine. Daniel was hunched over her back, tattoo gun in hand, as he permanently marked Julia's skin with her song. Black music notes covered her inflamed skin. But unlike what he'd done to the others, he wasn't just tattooing a stanza of the music. It looked as if he were tattooing the *entire composition*.

It was a sacrilege. All of it. But it didn't matter, because Rhys had gotten to Julia in time.

She was *alive.*

The two hours it had taken Rhys to reach her had been the worst of his life. He hadn't waited for backup before jumping in his car and speeding toward the cabin. His brothers followed in their vehicles right behind him. All Rhys had cared about was getting to Julia before Daniel killed her. Rhys had been an hour too late to save his mother's life. But he wouldn't fail Julia.

Joshua had mobilized the response team. The ambulances were on their way, as were a handful of agents from the Atlanta FBI field office.

Joshua and Sam remained out in the hallway, and outside were at least a dozen law enforcement officers from the Laurel Creek Sheriff's Department, which included a sharpshooter. Unfortunately, there were no windows in the room. It was up to Rhys to de-escalate the situation and get Julia away from Daniel. He assessed the room for dangers. Other than the tattoo kind, Rhys didn't see a gun.

Glock in hand, Rhys stalked into the room. Daniel moved faster than Rhys could have imagined. Before Rhys could apprehend him, Daniel swiped a butcher knife from the cart beside him and jumped to his feet. He dropped the tattoo gun and raised Julia's head up by the hair, putting the blade against the front of her throat.

Rhys pointed the gun at Daniel. "Fenske, put down the knife."

"Rhys?" Julia's voice was just barely audible underneath all the buzzing.

He wanted to go to her, to rip her out of the chair and carry her out in his arms. "I'm here, Julia," he called out. "Just hold on."

"I never thanked you, Rhys," Daniel said.

"Thanked me?"

Daniel's hands started shaking. A slow trickle of blood ran down Julia's neck, but she didn't move or make a sound. If she hadn't just whispered his name, he might have thought she was already gone.

"I tried so hard to protect her," Daniel said.

With Daniel holding the blade to Julia's throat, Rhys couldn't afford to say anything that would set him off. One deep slash to the carotid or jugular would kill her. "Protect her from who?"

"Protect her from *me*. You did what my letters and I couldn't. You got her to leave."

What Daniel was saying didn't make sense. "You're telling me you wrote the letters to scare her out of town?"

"I followed her, you know. I saw you kissing underneath the waterfall. She was supposed to be mine to protect. *Mine*. You took her from me. That's when the urges got worse. Do you know what it's like to want something so badly, it's all you think about?"

"Sure," Rhys said flippantly, even though inside he was seething. He hadn't taken Julia away from Daniel. She'd given herself to him willingly, just as he'd given himself to her. It was clear Daniel definitely wasn't playing with a full deck.

"If she hadn't left when she did, I don't think I could've stopped myself from hurting her."

"But she did leave." And Rhys had never been more grateful for that fact.

"As did the urges," Daniel said. His fingers tightened on the blade, turning them white. "But then she called a couple months ago, and I couldn't say no."

"Which made you angry." Rhys had to figure out a way to get Daniel to surrender. Right now, he couldn't take the risk that if he shot Daniel, the man wouldn't take down Julia with him. "Tell me about Diana Crain."

"Diana used to take cello lessons from me when she was a child. I got off the phone with Julia and went for a walk. Diana was crying hysterically. She was having one of her panic attacks. Baker hadn't picked her up from work. I offered to accompany her home. I hadn't intended to hurt her."

Funny how in Daniel's stories, he never meant to hurt the women. It was as if he wanted to see himself as a victim in all of it. But some things couldn't be excused.

"What changed?" Rhys asked.

"The urges returned. My mind was filled with images of Julia and my mother. I couldn't make it stop. And Diana wouldn't stop sobbing. No one was around, so I dragged her into the woods and I made her stop."

Julia whimpered and her fingers twitched.

Hold on a little longer, sweetheart.

It killed him to ignore her, but if he was going to convince Daniel to give himself up, he had to build a rapport with him first. "How did you make her stop?"

"I hit her until she passed out." There was no inflection to Daniel's voice, but like other serial killers Rhys had encountered in the past, there was a gleam in his eyes as if he were remembering the event with fondness. "Then I found a trash bag filled with empty beer cans, no doubt left behind by some teenagers after a party. I dumped the cans, slipped the bag over her face and tightened it. As her life force drained away, I realized the urge to kill Julia did too."

By claiming to be at the mercy of his urges and to excuse his behavior, he'd cast himself as a victim in the story while, at the same time, playing the hero who had saved Julia's life.

"Explain something for me," Rhys said. "If the murder was spur of the moment, why didn't we find any prints on the bag or on Diana?"

"I wore gloves. I had them on me just in case..."

"You'd already started preparing." Diana's murder might have been unplanned, but the fantasy was already on his mind when Daniel had walked out his door that night. When he'd stumbled upon a young woman with similar features to Julia, he'd been ready.

Daniel didn't acknowledge Rhys's statement. "After Diana died, the urges disappeared for a few days, but then they came back stronger than ever. I couldn't trust that I wouldn't harm Julia. I had to choose another in her place. This time, I'd make sure I did it right. Diana's body was hidden just like my father had hidden my mother's. My next kill would be found right away."

It took a moment for Rhys to process what Daniel had said and to put the pieces together. Daniel's father had killed his mother and had disposed of her where she had never been found. She hadn't abandoned her family. At least not willingly. "And the tattoo? What's its purpose?"

"If I left a piece of Julia on their bodies, they became Julia," he said as if it should be obvious to everyone. "She was safe. But it stopped working. It became clear that I no longer had a choice. I needed to kill Julia. Then my father..."

"Your father?" Rhys prodded.

"The urges come to me in his voice. He wants me to be like him. He talks in my head and tells me all the ways I should torture Julia. I had no other choice."

"No, you always had a choice. You still have a choice. Put down the knife, Daniel." Rhys used a tranquil tone. "You don't want to hurt Julia any more than you already have. I can help you. If you let Julia go and come with me, I'll take you to a place where you'll never be able to hurt anyone again. And then I'll personally see to it that your mother's body is found and that it's made public that your father killed her."

In the blink of an eye, the expression on Daniel's face changed. His pupils dilated like two full moons eating up the irises, and his lips twisted into a sneer.

"Out of everyone," Daniel spit out, "I would have thought that you would understand. My father is dead. He was never punished for his sins. Your mother was murdered, just like mine. Your mother's killer has gone unpunished, just like mine. Wouldn't you give anything to provide justice for her?"

Daniel the victim and Daniel the hero had been replaced by Daniel the villain. This Daniel wasn't going to be reasoned with.

Rhys had lost out on his opportunity to get him to surrender without force.

But he couldn't give up trying.

"You could have reported your mother's murder, if not when you were a kid, then when you became an adult," Rhys said. "You could have had yourself admitted to a psychiatric facility when you began having the urges. Instead, you killed six women. Where's the justice for them? Killing Julia won't bring justice to your mom. She's dead, Fenske. Nothing will bring her back. Do you think your mom would be proud of you? Your father killed one woman. You've killed six. I think she'd be horrified to know the monster you've become."

There was a brief spark of something in Daniel's gaze that led Rhys to believe he'd gotten through to him. But Daniel shook it off with the flick of his wrist. "I've accepted my fate. Have you accepted yours?" His smile terrified Rhys. "If you kill me, you'll never get to learn the truth."

"What truth?"

Julia gurgled as blood dripped off her neck onto the floor. In that moment, Rhys knew that Daniel would alter his MO to fit the situation. With the tattoo on her back, he'd completed his signature ritual. Rhys had run out of time.

Daniel's smile widened as he pressed the blade deeper into Julia's skin. "About why your mother was killed."

Rhys's pulse skittered out of control. He didn't have a choice anymore. "And I suppose you know."

"I do. If you shoot me, I'll take the secret with me. You'll never find out who killed her. Can you live with that?"

Rhys took his eyes off Daniel for a second to gaze at Julia. There wasn't a question. "Yes."

With a clear shot to the head, Rhys seized his chance. Daniel toppled to the floor, but not before a look of peace washed over his face. The blade clanked on the concrete. It had been over so quickly, he'd never had the opportunity to use the knife. Julia lay motionless on the chair, blood pooling under her neck and staining the ends of her hair red.

Rhys ran to her. "It's all clear," he shouted to his brothers. "Get the paramedics here. Now." He tore the Velcro restraints off her wrists and ankles.

Sam and Joshua marched into the room, Sam shutting off the tattoo machine and Joshua confirming Daniel was dead. The front door opened, and numerous officers poured into the house to make sure the area was secure.

Knowing it would hurt Julia, Rhys didn't roll her over. He brushed her hair out of her face. Her eyes fluttered but remained closed. As a flurry of activity abounded, he removed his shirt and pressed it against the cuts on her throat to stem the bleeding. Then he carefully lifted her into his arms in a fireman's hold, rested her over his shoulder and carried her out of the house.

"Rhys?" Julia asked listlessly. "I don't remember you ever carrying me like this in the past. That must mean… Are you really here?"

Relieved to hear her sweet voice, he breathed out a sigh. "Yeah, sweetheart. I'm really here. It's all over, Julia. Daniel can't hurt you anymore."

The ambulance's sirens grew louder as it drove up the road and came into view. Rhys strode toward it with purpose. She needed care, the kind he couldn't give her. But Rhys didn't know how to let her go.

"Rhys, he's the Composer," she said, lifting her head and looking at him with bloodshot eyes. "He witnessed his father murder his mother. He was crazy. How could I not have known?"

If only he had seen through Daniel's act. None of this would've happened. It was as if all his darkest fears had been realized. "He fooled everyone. Not only you. I'm so sorry you had to go through this, Julia. I'm sorry I didn't figure it out before he took you."

The paramedics rushed toward them.

"Careful," Rhys warned, "she's got slices on the front of her neck, and her back—"

"We've got her," one of them said, reassuring him. "You need to let us take it from here."

Everything inside of Rhys screamed at him to keep her in his arms. He worried if he didn't, he'd never have the chance again. But she needed medical care far more than she needed him right now.

He transferred her over to a paramedic, who gently placed her on a gurney.

Rhys went with them as they rolled her into the back of the ambulance.

"Rhys? I love you so much," Julia cried. "Don't leave me, okay? Promise never to leave me."

The words were there on his tongue. *I love you.* But he couldn't get himself to say them, and he couldn't get himself to join her in the back of the ambulance.

And as it drove away, he pressed a hand to his chest.

It felt empty inside.

As if she'd taken his heart with her.

Chapter Nineteen

Rhys slipped the sunglasses over his eyes as he walked up his father's front steps. The last week in Atlanta had been the longest in his life.

Since the ambulance had driven away with Julia inside of it, he hadn't had a moment's rest. He'd spent hours at Daniel's childhood home processing the crime scene, followed by phone calls and paperwork and visits to the victims' families. There were press conferences and interviews with the media.

A search team had been formed to recover Daniel's mother, but so far, they hadn't found anything. Since Daniel had died before he could share her location, it was highly unlikely they'd ever find her.

Time had gotten away from him, but Julia had never left his thoughts. All he'd wanted to do was get work out of the way and return to her side. But whenever he'd been about to call her, he'd found himself pulled into another meeting.

How had he survived without Julia for twelve years when now he felt as if he wouldn't survive another minute? He wanted to wake up every morning beside her. Wanted to see her round with their child and sit on her porch swing to watch the fireworks explode over the mountains on Independence Day.

But he'd blown his chance. He'd almost lost Julia, and instead of telling her how much he loved her, he'd ghosted her. There was no good excuse for it. She'd never forgive him. And he'd never forgive himself.

After finishing his report at the FBI's Atlanta field office, he'd looked at his calendar and realized it was Friday night. Without a conscious thought, he'd gotten into his car and drove the hour and half to his father's house. There were times when a man needed his family, and right now was one of those times. The absence of his brothers' cars signaled they weren't there yet, but he was actually glad, because that's not whose guidance he sought.

Normally, he'd use his key and let himself in the house, but today he knocked on the door. His shoulders dropped, some of his tension easing, as he heard his father's footsteps nearing the door. He hadn't realized until that moment how much he'd feared his dad permanently retreating back into his workshop again and avoiding the land of the living.

His father opened the door and waved him inside. He looked the same as last week, clean-shaven and dressed for dinner. "Rhys. Come in. What's with the glasses?"

Rhys removed them, showing off the dark circles and bags under his eyes.

His dad cringed. "Ah. Rough week, I take it?"

He followed his dad to the living room and took a seat on the couch as his dad sat in his old recliner. "I assume you heard?" The house smelled like the charcoal from the barbecue. He found it oddly comforting.

"Mm. It's all over the news, and Sam filled me in on what wasn't reported." Griffin sat back and kicked up his feet. "How's Julia?"

Well, his dad quickly got right to the heart of the matter, didn't he?

"I don't know," Rhys admitted. "I haven't seen her. I got busy at work."

"Too busy to check on your girl?"

Was that what she was to him? Because she felt like more, and yet, he didn't have the right to even call her his. She'd made it clear she wanted him. She'd even told him she loved him, although she'd been in pain and half-conscious at the time. He was the one who'd kept insisting they could never work. "I messed up. But she's not my girl."

"Not your girl?" His father shook his head. "Do you always lie to yourself or just when you're too chicken to go for what you really want? I thought I raised you to be smarter than that."

Rhys jumped up from the couch. "You didn't raise me at all!" he shouted. "You don't get to take any credit for the man I've turned into."

His dad didn't appear to be offended by Rhys's outburst. He actually smiled. "Good. You're finally ready to have it out. You're right. I've earned that anger. But you deserve more. And I should've given it to you. I failed. As a husband. A sheriff. A father. I thought if I solved your mother's murder, she'd forgive me for not being here to protect her. But instead, I forgot to protect the rest of my family. I know I can never get those years back, but it would mean the world to me if you'd let me be there for you now."

Rhys had waited twenty years for those words. He'd spent so long being angry at his dad that he almost didn't know what it was like to live without it.

Rhys dragged a chair from the dining room table and set it in front of his father. He deserved to know what happened. "Before I shot Fenske, he told me he had information on Mom's murder. I had to choose between that information and Julia, and I chose Julia."

"As you should have."

Rhys hadn't anticipated that reaction. "You're not upset?"

His dad leaned forward. "I'm upset that someone kidnapped your girl, but no, I'm not upset I might have lost out on a lead in your mom's case. Who knows if Fenske was telling the truth? But even if he was, Julia is far more precious than some information that won't bring your mom back. If you're ever ready, you and I can sit down with my files and figure out if there is a connection between Daniel and your mom's murder. But if you're never ready, that's okay too."

Maybe that day would come eventually, but for Rhys, it wouldn't be anytime soon. Because his father was right.

To Rhys, Julia was more precious than the air that he breathed. He couldn't live without her, and even if he could, he didn't want to. There was always a risk he could lose her, but he'd rather take that risk and love her than live without her. "I saw you cry. It scared me. I loved Julia so much that it would have killed me if something had happened to her. I thought we'd both be better off if we broke up before either one of us got hurt."

His dad's brows dipped. "Seems like all you did was hurt both of you."

"How do I fix it?" he asked.

"I can't tell you how to do that."

"We can help." Sam stepped into the room with Joshua right behind him. "We'll tell you exactly how to get Julia back."

JULIA LAID THE bouquet of white roses in the grass on top of Daniel's grave. Only a handful of people, all of them from the symphony, had shown up to pay their respects at his funeral today. She expected others had been wary of being associated with a serial killer. Her parents thought it was improper for her to arrange his funeral and order his tombstone, but he had no one else. There had been a time when she'd known what that was like. Maybe that's what had drawn the two of them together.

With the others now gone, she finally permitted herself to cry. In her mind, Daniel Fenske was two different people. There had been the monster responsible for tormenting her for years who had viciously murdered six women and had planned on adding her to the total. And then there was the Daniel who had nurtured her love for the violin and had been the one stable adult figure in her life since becoming a teenager. How was that for irony?

True to form, rather than fly out to comfort their only child who'd been nearly killed, her parents had taken the opportunity to try to convince her to leave Laurel Creek. Career-wise it made sense. Because the board of trustees had failed to hire a new assistant conductor since the previous one left last year, the symphony was currently without one and therefore was on a brief hiatus while the board searched for a new one to take Daniel's place.

Thankfully, the symphony's contracts had the option for its musicians to either find alternate employment during this time or remain paid employees during the shutdown. Julia had a few weeks to decide whether to remain with the Laurel Creek Symphony or move on and do something new with her life. What she'd never do again is live her parents' dreams. It was time for her to find a new one.

Julia turned at the sound of soft footsteps brushing through the grass behind her. Her heart skipped a beat as the last person she expected to see approached. Wearing a black suit and carrying a few long-stemmed white roses, Rhys strolled toward her.

At the sight of him, hope sparked within her, and her traitorous heart skipped a beat. She hadn't heard from him all week. That first day in the hospital, she'd kept checking the door to the room, eagerly anticipating his arrival. When he didn't show or call, she'd assumed he was too busy with the case. A couple of other FBI special agents had come by to take her statement about her kidnapping and the hours spent strapped to the tattoo chair. After she got home, she'd gotten visits from her friend Ellie, Sam and Joshua, even Griffin. They'd all told her to be patient, that Rhys would come around, but as the days passed, she'd lost faith.

The last place she had ever expected to see him was at Daniel's grave. "What are you doing here?"

When his gaze fell to the bandage on her neck, his eyes narrowed and his jaw tightened. She instinctively put her hand over it. The cuts Daniel had given her hadn't required stitches, but until they closed, the doctors advised she keep them covered. The tattoo was permanent, and maybe someday, she'd have it removed, but while she despised the manner in which she'd gotten it, the tattooed music was a part of her. It reminded her that she was a survivor.

Rhys shook off whatever had been going through his head, and his expression softened. He laid his flowers beside hers on the ground. "Sorry I'm late.

I tried to get here before the funeral service started, but I was held up by a phone call from work."

She turned away from him. If he'd come here to make sure she knew it was over between them, she'd already gotten the message. "It must have been a long phone call, considering I haven't heard from you all week."

"I'm sorry," he said contritely. "There's no good excuse for waiting this long to see you, and if I could do it differently, I would."

His apology surprised her. She'd expected him to list off all the things in his life that took priority over her. If he wasn't here to officially break things off between them, why was he? "You were going to attend Daniel's funeral? Why?" she asked, spinning to face him.

"To be here for you." He took a giant step toward her and took her hand. "I know how difficult it must be for you. You loved him."

Her resistance crumbled. It always would when it came to Rhys. "I want to hate him, I do, but I can't."

"I wouldn't expect any different." His thumb brushed over her hand, making her shiver. "I know you think it's a flaw, but your big heart is one of the things I love about you."

Love?

"I don't believe it's a flaw anymore. I still believe the best in people, and if they disappoint me, that's not a reflection on me." Rhys had taught her that and he'd been right.

"I'm glad. Because it would be a shame if you became as jaded as the rest of us."

She gazed into his hazel eyes. "Is that what you are? Jaded?"

He caressed his knuckles down her cheekbone. "I thought I was until you came back into my life."

Her chest filled with warmth. "And now?"

"And now I believe in the possibility."

"The possibility of what?" she asked.

He pulled her closer. "Of me and you."

"What are you saying, Rhys?" Her big heart was beating in triple time.

His dimples made an appearance as he grinned. "I don't want to do this here. Not now. Not today. Can I take you out tomorrow night?"

She heard the words, but it took a moment to process them. "You mean, on a date?"

He chuckled. "Yes, Julia. On a date."

She smiled. "I'd like that."

"I'll pick you up at your house at seven," he said. *What did one wear on a date with Rhys Keller?*

THIRTY HOURS AFTER saying goodbye at the cemetery, Rhys held her hand as they walked through the forest to their waterfall. Knowing Daniel had spied on them and then used the area as a dumping ground for his victims made their return to their special spot bittersweet. But she refused to allow Daniel to taint the beautiful memories she and Rhys had created there. The waterfall belonged to them.

The evening was hot and humid, but Julia didn't mind. She barely even noticed.

Because there, by the bank of their waterfall, white twinkling lights draped the branches of the trees. Underneath lay a square blanket, large enough for the both of them, with a banquet of food spread out upon it. Soft piano music played in the background— Rachmaninoff, if she wasn't mistaken—and a bottle of champagne was sticking out of a tall metal bucket. It was as if Rhys had plucked this fairy tale right from her fantasies. It completely stole her breath.

Her mouth dropped open as she took it all in. "This is beautiful. You did all this yourself?"

"I'd love to take all the credit, but no," he said sheepishly. "I had some help from Sam and Joshua."

She threw her arms around Rhys's neck. "Who knew they had it in them?"

He placed his hands on her waist. "Julia, twelve years ago, I made the biggest mistake of my life when I lied to you. You were right. I thought I was protecting you when I was really only protecting myself. I'd like the chance to make it up to you. I've spoken with Joshua, and he says there are openings in the sheriff's department."

It was everything she'd ever wanted. What she and Rhys had talked about all those years ago. She'd never thought she'd have the opportunity.

"You'd give up your job for me and work for Sheriff Pearce?" she asked. The city council had reviewed the sheriff's actions, including his dismissal of the guard watching her, and determined he had done nothing wrong.

"My job is based out of Atlanta. Your home is in Laurel Creek. And my home is wherever you are."

A happy tear slid down her cheek. "I feel the same way. When I was in Europe, I missed my home, which is why I came back to Laurel Creek. But I realized the house, the town—they never felt like home until you were in it. I've been thinking of going to school to get my degree in music education. There are a few schools in Atlanta."

His lips hovered over hers. "What if we kept your house in Laurel Creek and came back on the weekends to spend Sabbath with our family?"

"I love that idea." Her pulse raced as she processed his words. "Wait, *our* family? Don't you mean, *your* family?"

He shook his head and dropped to one knee. "I meant what I said. I have loved you for more than half my life. I bought this ring twelve years ago. Even though I never gave it to you, it's always been yours... just like my heart. In case you haven't figured it out, I love you. Julia Harcourt, will you do me the honor of marrying me and becoming an official member of the Keller family?"

She fell to her knees with tears in her eyes, and if she wasn't mistaken, his eyes were a bit misty too. "Yes, Rhys Keller. I'll marry you."

His lips covered hers with the promise of forever, and after several minutes, they were both breathless.

He smiled at her and gestured to the blanket. "Lie with me and tell me your dreams."

She had a better idea. "How about I show you instead?"

* * * * *

*Look for more books in Shelly Bell's
Shield of Honor miniseries coming
soon from Harlequin Intrigue!*

COMING NEXT MONTH FROM

ⒽHARLEQUIN
INTRIGUE

#2157 MAVERICK DETECTIVE DAD
Silver Creek Lawmen: Second Generation • by Delores Fossen
When Detective Noah Ryland and Everly Monroe's tragic pasts make them targets of a vigilante killer, they team up to protect her young daughter and stop the murders. But soon their investigation unleashes a series of vicious attacks...along with reigniting the old heat between them.

#2158 MURDER AT SUNSET ROCK
Lookout Mountain Mysteries • by Debra Webb
A ransacked house suggests that Olivia Ballard's grandfather's death was no mere accident. Deputy Detective Huck Monroe vows to help her uncover the truth. But as dark secrets surrounding Olivia's family are exposed, she'll have to trust the man who broke her heart to stay alive.

#2159 SHROUDED IN THE SMOKIES
A Tennessee Cold Case Story • by Lena Diaz
Former detective Adam Trent is stunned to learn his cold case victim is alive. But Skylar Montgomery is still very much in danger—and desperate for Adam's help. Their investigation leads them to one of Chattanooga's most powerful families...and a vicious web of mystery, intrigue and murder.

#2160 TEXAS BODYGUARD: WESTON
San Antonio Security • by Janie Crouch
Security Specialist Weston Patterson risks everything to keep his charges safe. But protecting wealthy Kayleigh Delacruz is his biggest challenge yet. She doesn't want a bodyguard. But as the kidnapping threat grows, she'll do anything—even trust Weston's expertise—to survive.

#2161 DIGGING DEEPER
by Amanda Stevens
When Thora Graham awakens inside a coffin-like box with no memory of how she got there, Deputy Police Chief Will Dresden, the man she left fifteen years ago, follows the clues to save her life. Their twisted reunion becomes a race against time to stop a serial killer's vengeful scheme.

#2162 K-9 HUNTER
by Cassie Miles
Piper Comstock and her dog, Izzy, live a solitary, peaceful life. Until her best friend is targeted by an assassin. US Marshal Gavin McQueen knows the truth— a witness in protection is compromised. It's dangerous to recruit a civilian to help with the investigation. But is the danger to Piper's life...or Gavin's heart?

YOU CAN FIND MORE INFORMATION ON UPCOMING HARLEQUIN TITLES, FREE EXCERPTS AND MORE AT HARLEQUIN.COM.

HICNM0623

HARLEQUIN
PLUS

Try the best multimedia subscription service for romance readers like you!

Read, Watch and Play.

Experience the easiest way to get the romance content you crave.

Start your **FREE TRIAL** at
www.harlequinplus.com/freetrial.